# The Mayfly

------------

# Robin Eddy

*Tarnhelm Books*

*TARNHELM BOOKS (UK)*


*The Mayfly* first published
in October 2006

2nd edition November 2006
3rd edition April 2007
4th edition August 2009
5th edition August 2011


ISBN 978-0-9565289-3-3

*To you is given a body more graceful than other animals,*
*to you power of apt and various movements,*
*to you most sharp and delicate senses,*
*to you wit, reason, memory,*
*like an immortal god.*

(Leon Battista Alberti)


*If an innocence was lost here, it was not the boy's…*


*Nothing is invented in* Death in Venice.
*The sinister gondolier, Tadzio and his family,*
*all that and anything else you like,*
*they were all there.*

(Thomas Mann)


*The idea for* The Mayfly *came down to me*
*as if it were some kind of automatic*
*writing, and I merely the medium.*
*I wrote it in six weeks, and*
*wept when it was done.*

(R. E.)

*In Memoriam Benjamin Britten*

who wrote on 4th March 1976:

*"It was very good of you to send me
the typed copy of 'The Mayfly'.
Your description of your novel
sounds very sympathetic."*

# *I.*

The two candles on the lectern to his left flickered and smoked with a sweet waxy aroma, mingling, through the vast stone perspectives of the Choir, with a subtler perfume, which originated perhaps from the flowers arranged in great urns before the altar, from polish, or something less tangible: a distillation, in another dimension, of ancient stone, wood, music and prayer, to delight the senses.

*What was he doing here?* For as long as he could remember, he had tried to leave the world to its own devices, had strained away beyond the bounds of convention, seeking at all costs to avoid an existence in the rut. Up to now, this had brought him only despair more often than not, but today (it was not just a hunch – he recognised the signs), *today* was all set to become one of those watersheds that single a man out for an irreversible experience, by tilting his precarious world on its head. He smelt his own fear already.

Organ notes came pulsing through the building, answered by the distant chiming of a clock, and this mysterious music seized hold of him, like some unexpected magnetism poised to draw him down from the canon's stall on the south side, where they had placed him, to appear on a stage and participate in a specially created drama quite alien to the normal routines of sanctity here.

No longer did he see slender Gothic pillars soaring into the complex tracery above, but a magical forest whose trees reached up to entwine their foliage, out of which peeped small creatures with the grotesque faces much loved by medieval sculptors, full of humour and menace. For a moment or two, the vision had him in its grip, like some virus possessed of unaccustomed and irrational power.

Escape from this place was no longer possible: the little knots of worshippers, seated up behind the choir stalls by the vergers, were trapped in their places by the arrival of a robed procession, led by two lines of choirboys issuing from the arch in the massive organ screen beyond the lectern, followed by the men and, finally, the priests. The solemnity of their measured slowness quite dispelled any idea that they might be creatures come to haunt the forest, for his frivolous mind was instead serving them up as potential extras in one of his opera designs.

As though activated by some unseen clockwork, the boys on each side filed into the front row of the stalls, the men into the one behind. With a synchronism rendered impersonal by its frequent practice, all faced towards the altar, then bowed and turned inwards, while the organist brought his improvisation to a neat conclusion. And the observer waited expectantly for the event to happen, whatever it should be.

A priest on the far side invited the people to confess their sins, and everyone knelt. The man placed his palms on the cool wood of the ancient stall, and, before his very eyes, a shaft of the sun descended from a window high above, like a stage spot switched on, making a pool of light before the altar rail, a tantalising reminder, in this sombre place, of the hot but tender Spring afternoon which he had left outside, bright and burgeoning amid its new foliage. He felt his heart beating more quickly.

The choir began to sing a psalm, its verses tossed from one side to the other. Above and beyond the men's deeper harmonies, the boys' voices rose and fell like fountains, causing the stranger to look across at those in the front row of the stalls opposite. The sun had gone in again, and the choristers now appeared to be overlaid by a kind of defensive outer shell, as though they were not human beings, in their dark-blue cassocks, immaculately laundered surplices and ruffs, but automata who sang, sat, stood and knelt to order, resembling those shiny figurines one came across in china shops – young lads, most of whose heads scarcely rose above the ledge on which they put their music. Maybe these children were hard, proud and snobbish, conscious of their eliteness. Indeed, with their slicked-down hair and monkish little faces, they looked already half-way to becoming porcelain angels, not the sort to watch TV or enjoy jokes or have a fight. No, they came here to make exquisite music and, at the end of the service, they would be taken away and shut up like pet mice until they were needed again. *So, why was the newcomer on tenterhooks?*

To his eye, the carved wooden canopies above the canons' stalls resembled a stage set, until he remarked that each statue of priest or saint in its niche reposed beneath that dust of ages which might even have the capacity to cushion, beneath layers of caution, a casual member of the congregation from pain and harm: past mistakes were not to be repeated, especially where closeness with another person might be involved.

Again a voice broke across his thoughts. A priest, standing before the lectern, let the words of the lesson soar like an incantation into the vaulting above. To the man's left, the other priests were slumped in their seats in apparent boredom. For whom was this elaborate charade being staged, then? Surely not for a mere visitor, unattuned to the holy mysteries of this place? Was everyone else in this great building stuck fast in a groove, and was *he* the only one present to see it like that? The lesson ended on a dry-sounding echo, and the atmosphere of torpor was suddenly broken, as the choir rose to sing the Magnificat.

Glancing between the backs of two choirmen immediately in front of him, the man found that his roving gaze had missed a significant detail: in the line of boys opposite, those at each end, - the senior trebles evidently, - wore a black hooded cloak fastened by a chain and medallion; and the senior to the right was a tallish lad with a fringe of fluffy brown hair, a pale face and a manner of standing that distinguished him from his fellows: instead of holding his head up to sing, he kept it down, looking out under his brows. Nor did he, like the other boys, observe the discipline of keeping still, but fidgeted with his hands, as though nervous.

The stranger decided that he must have been blind. Why had his eye not lit upon this boy before? Perhaps because he was the furthest away, and in gloom. As if a spell had been cast, the sun's spotlight returned to the pavement just in front of him, favouring the chorister with its reflected radiance. Now *he* looked about him, and his glance passed over the stranger, momentarily checking its course before moving on. The observer just had time to notice that the eyes were large and dark, the expression both sweet and grave; and it dwelt upon him with the quality of a signal, like a face in a painting. His curious expectancy now yielded to a vague sense of disquiet: where was the rational apparatus which might explain how or why he should suddenly be thus affected? The boy's glance had set off some mystic inner machinery within him which had long since fallen into disuse. His wayward brain served him up the beautiful boy in Thomas Mann's story, and his hapless admirer. Like Aschenbach's experience, it was course quite absurd, but not entirely without dignity. There was in him now a strange throbbing that he knew would take a long time to die down again.

The music came to an end, one of the priests ascended the steps of the pulpit and began to pronounce a text. The man's wilful and curious eye swept again along the choir stalls opposite, but the boys were hunched up, their faces mostly out of sight. The senior on the far end was staring down, perhaps quite oblivious to words in which he might find no comfort or purpose, and unaware that he was under observation.

In his time spent in this town, the newcomer had often looked up at the great cathedral church on its ridge, like the upturned hull of a stranded grey ship, but, apart from one quick, freezing visit back in the winter, had never set foot inside the place. Today, however, the Minster had stood out against the brilliant sky, its towers claiming his attention as never before, challenging him to ascend and admire. The stone glowed in the sunlight, every detail of tracery and carving impinged upon his vision, as though he were in that heightened state of receptivity which attends a fever. Perhaps he *was* feverish, mentally, emotionally even, to believe that some external force had delivered him into the sacred core of this place, where a boy's momentary gaze would set all kinds of ancient chords sounding deep within him. He could pass it off as merely the promise of coolness which had lured him here, but then, once inside, the need to avoid the tourists wandering about, guidebook in hand, had urged him towards the screen which, beneath its huge organ case, blocked the way to the Choir. From that moment, there was no turning back: a verger had asked if he intended to stay for Evensong and, in a trice, he, who had never paid more than lip-service to the trappings of Christianity, had been beckoned into a conspiracy that he as yet had no inkling of, positioned like a celebrity in the very heart of the building, where holy things were sung and done. Whatever the future consequences of today's action might be, they would not be his fault...

The Canon ended his dry little homily and announced the closing hymn, - "God moves in a mysterious way" – the men and boys rose, followed by the sparse congregation, and the man's dæmon made him look across at that senior boy again, to verify that he had been dreaming, that choirboys did not exchange glances with total strangers in a gathering of the devout. And so it was: he did not look across this time, which, to the observer's surprise, filled him with a curious and unaccountable wistfulness.

For the sake of sanity, he needed a logical context in which to site this boy: if anyone here was clearly aware of the world about him, and human, it was he, whose body-language and general appearance suggested a maturer agenda, freed from the repetitions and rigours of his life in the Choir School: a young man, whose development might be full of promise. So, now, the man's prophesied watershed moment had arrived, from the least expected quarter, and he had to admit to himself that he was interested, intrigued even! As if to lend a touch of legality to his unruly thoughts, one sang Cowper's incomparable words:

> *"Ye fearful saints, fresh courage take;*
> *the clouds ye so much dread*
> *are big with mercy, and shall break*
> *in blessings on your head."*

After the Blessing, the choir repeated its clockwork routine, filing into the central aisle between the stalls, then turned about and, led by the verger as before, set off in the double line out under the organ screen, just as it had come in. The dark lad at the front, with his fair-haired opposite number on this side, walked with short rocking steps. He could only be about thirteen, yet, towering over the little boys behind him, he looked older. His new-found admirer (what word would now fit him better?) watched him intently, willing him to look up, and prove that the magic dust lay upon the keen spectator after all, that he had witnessed an electric spark between the two of them.

What happened next was a moment of pure drama. His lad, (for already there was an urgent possessiveness in him), turned his head a little to the left as he drew level, and his dark eyes unmistakeably singled the stranger out again: *this is for you; take it away as a gift from me.* And, as if to seal the compact, there was the faintest suspicion of a flush rising in his face, while the man's own cheeks burned in answer. The organ notes rang out, the procession continued on its way, but *he who had witnessed* was conscious only of a heat within, a joy, a knowledge that a message had passed between them, and been mutually understood.

When the last priest had disappeared through the arch, and the man knelt down with the rest of the congregation, there was the vestige of a smile on his lips. For what had seemed unreal, but a moment ago, had become reality indeed. The soft music made a crescendo, and a fiery and jubilant toccata began to ripple through the Minster. The boy had gone, but he had left a glow inside his secret beholder and, with it, a strange and welcome awareness of inner bonds being loosened, of a line stepped over even, of a calling forth from a deep dark slumber to some enterprise, as yet unfocussed and unhoped-for. Was it possible that such a thing could happen only within the confines of this ancient and venerable church? The man, feeling himself a stranger no more, carefully folded the printed service card, pocketed it and went out of the Minster like one blessed.

*

With Fillingham at his side, he led the procession up the south Choir aisle, full of wonder at the daring thing he had just done. All right, so he had recently taken to 'trawling the conga' for an interesting face, for anyone who looked a bit different from the usual daily collection of old dears (mostly ancient women, ready to pop their clogs any moment).

The man had certainly been looking across, more than once in the service. That couldn't be just accidental, could it? At first he thought it might be another of those public-school talent-spotters who went touting for customers round prep schools. But the man had been wearing a light-weight grey suit which didn't look English, and he was handsome, though his expression was rather sad. His eyes were always on the move, taking everything in. How old? Fair hair beginning to go a little thin, but he wasn't at all wrinkly. Under forty.

When the procession reached the vestries, where its strict formation dissolved into the mêlée of men and boys disrobing, a cold common-sense overtook him. The bloke would never show up again. Probably just some foreigner, German most likely, passing through, and who hadn't seen the inside of an English cathedral before. Maybe he was knocked over by it. Pity if he were to vanish now, because he had something attractive about him that wasn't easy to put your finger on. Why would he notice a mere grubby choirboy looking over at him? If only he could slip out, here and now, instead of having to wait till they were taken back to school, he might just catch a glimpse of the man. But then, things like that simply didn't happen…

When he turned it over in his head later on after lights out, he was surprised and not a little shocked to find how much this thing was still lodged in his mind. He wasn't usually bothered about other people, and certainly not in this strange sort of way. God, was he going romantic? He'd begun to notice something affecting him these days, which certainly wasn't just physical. Crazy, how things seemed to be stirring up inside him, as if he was going to turn from a mere prep-school boarder into a monster any minute, and burst through this cosy environment into the world waiting for him outside. He wanted to stretch himself, flex his muscles and taste real freedom for the first time. He desperately needed someone to talk to…

*

His head spinning, the man walked through beneath the arch which closed the Minster Yard, and took refuge in a tea-room round the corner. An event, which he had in a way foreseen, and for which the omens must already have been in place when he set foot in the building, had momentarily knocked him off his perch. But what did this apparent converse of eyes, this piece of theatre *mean?* Anyone else would have shrugged it off, forgotten it in an instant, put it down to a trick of the light inside the Minster.

His first reaction was all too typical: abandon his work here, pack up and flee back to the safe anonymity of his place abroad, where he would be cured of this unnameable folly. His second thought, however, was, as so often the case with him, quite opposed to the first: this encounter must be put to the test, to see if it was simply a hallucination, a dream in broad daylight, or a special gift. As he attempted to find a rationale, he was bombarded with a barrage of questions – what and why? how could this be, and what should he do about it? – all of which were troublesome, and offering no comforting or reassuring answers. In the thick of it, he was the last person to be analysing his odd experience with that child… And yet, the strange warm feeling remained real.

He descended the ancient street to the lower town and, reaching his rooms, picked up *Death in Venice*, flung himself into an easy chair and spent the next hour or two immersed in the text, desperate to know if such a thing could really happen outside the pages of Thomas Mann, and yet be somehow acceptable. By the time he wearily got up, it seemed that he had at last the makings of an answer.

*

*"O Lamb of God, that takest away the sins of the world, have mercy."* Boys' and men's voices were blending on either side of him, as he stood behind a long line of communicants on the pavement of the centre aisle, the congregation being larger for the Sunday Eucharist. Ahead, before the high altar, vestments shone and candles glittered, priests were mumbling the ancient formulæ as they dispensed the bread and wine at the altar rails, the people were shuffling slowly forward, and he was aware of the sweat trickling down his body, as it always used to do at this moment in the service when, as a schoolboy he left his seat, self-conscious and awkward, to go up before the One from whom no secrets were hidden.

Urged on by an inner curiosity, he had returned to the arena, the very heart of the Minster again, just half a week since that first Evensong, intending to approach all this objectively; but the sumptuousness of the setting, the soft organ accompaniment to the chanting of the choir, carried him away, as though he was no longer planted on the stone floor between the stalls, but hovering on some new and delectable wavelength to Heaven.

There he stood, the chorister who had caught his attention a few days ago. People who looked promising at a distance – actors on a stage, say – were often all too apt to disappoint when seen at close quarters, where an ugly feature might assume dominance. To his astonishment, the choirboy was, if anything, more perfect to the eye from close to, than when seen from the stall opposite. The sweetness of his pale face beneath its fringe of brown hair, and the purity of his skin were qualities one might expect to find in a girl. At this range one could see his eyes properly: dark grey. He kept his mouth slightly open, even when he was not singing, and the white teeth showed between full, fresh lips like those of an *amorino*. The admirer was charmed. Why should he not be?

The queue in front of him surged forward a few feet, taking him beyond the end of the stalls, but the sensation did not desert him: that the sight of a mere thirteen-year-old lad in cloak, cassock and surplice could so affect a man would seem ridiculous if viewed in a vacuum, but here, for a few moments at least, amid the pomp of the service, he allowed himself the wicked luxury of pretending that they were in St Mark's basilica, that he was playing Aschenbach to his Tadzio, and that, if only in spirit, they might one day tread part of their life's path together.

The man reached the altar rail and knelt, his body cold and clammy, as if in a tomb. Far away behind him, they were singing the Communion hymn, whose beauty echoed through the massive building. His hands trembled as he held them up to receive the wafer.

*"The Body of our Lord Jesus Christ, preserve thy body and soul unto everlasting life."*

But the fond one had surely reached his own vision of paradise already in this place!

*"Drink this…"*

He took the chalice, the priest opened his hands in a gesture of fellowship, and the sweat broke on the communicant's brow as he realised that the choir had been the first to take Communion, the dark-haired boy among them, so that the Cup, from which he now sipped, was being shared with *him*, who sang so sweetly with the others, behind his back.

He got up, turned and began the long walk back, guilty at heart, and all too aware of a sin that should already have been offered up and absolved. As he raised his eyes, the gloom of the sanctuary lightened, shafts of sunlight pierced the cloud outside and came through the south clerestory high above, making glowing windows of colour on the floor which he trod. The burden lifted, he felt that a question had somehow been answered, his confidence restored. The avenue of people along whom he passed, the double banks of carved pews, the organ on its screen ahead – all this which, a moment before, would have crowded in on him, became instead a path of excitement and, yes, triumph.

The choir had finished singing and were seated. As he drew level with the first of the stalls, he gave a quick, self-conscious look to the right, where *he* sat staring across to the other side. For a full second their eyes met, without either of them flinching, then the boy calmly lowered his gaze, and his admirer continued back to his place.

But his composure was gone, and as he climbed the wooden steps to the rear stalls, he stumbled, his foot hitting the riser with a force that made the space around him echo. He knelt, placing his hands on

the comforting cool ledge of medieval oak in front of him, his eyes
fixed on the broad back of the bass in front. The lad, (now directly
across from him, for the man had chosen a better viewpoint, right
behind the choir), must have heard, and perhaps seen, his
gaucheness, and he could not bear to look up and suffer the
amusement which might be in that face.

The notion of being in thrall to someone else brought him close
to despair. It had never worked, in the past. Staring down at the floor
of the aisle where the windows of sunlight spaced at regular intervals
had gone pale and ghostly, he was tempted to think that this church,
for all the beauty of its form and its music, might be given over to
nothing more than a caricaturing of religion, with the endless
succession of prayers, hymns, psalms, lessons and sermons. How did
*he* survive all this repetitiveness, that special boy whose gaze had
answered the man's with such openness, grace and seriousness,
confirming that there was indeed a growing understanding between
them? This was an experience which the observer had not sought nor
found in years, but he was sure that *he* knew the truth of it also: that,
as the admirer, he had returned here only for *his* sake.

Fired now by his temerity, he raised his eyes and looked over to
the *cantoris* stalls where the chorister knelt. A priest had already
begun the closing prayers, the service was nearly done. The boy's
head was bowed, one could not see his face, but his hands rested on
the ledge, in full view: they were long and slender, pale like the
hands of a statue, and beautiful in repose. But then a more mundane
thought entered the man's head: how did this boy cope with life in
the boarding house? As a senior, would he have learnt all about the
hunting instinct, about the sweet vice which renewed itself whenever
and wherever boys were living together in a tight, closed community,
where young flowering manhood was balanced against the glories of
Tallis and Byrd, unfolding to one's delighted ear?

One fact which now moved to the forefront of his mind was that
it fell to him, as the adult in the matter, to make the decision,
however painful. In his (few) past relationships, when it was clearly
pointless to continue, he had made a clean break. It was now a
question of not getting himself embroiled in this game of looks, of
nipping in the bud his interest in the choirboy opposite (and his
evident reciprocal curiosity). It was as if Mother was urging him to
remember that the virtues of manly decency and restraint must be
brought to bear.

He could have tried to pray for forgiveness and strength, if his heart were not suddenly so bitter, his mind so full of alarm. As the organ cut across the silent seconds after the Blessing, and the congregation rose, the boys were already filing out of their stalls. The two black-cloaked seniors at the front were facing the altar, then *he*, with the fair-haired boy, bowed stiffly and, like an infidel at Mecca, the man witnessed something he had just declared forbidden: they turned, and as they did so the tall dark chorister looked round at him, slowly, deliberately, without any trace of shyness or embarrassment, before leading the procession westward to the screen. The doors were open now, the verger preceded them with his staff, the organist's improvisation worked up to a purposeful climax which left one note exposed, and the choir, as it went out through the arch, began the processional psalm. *He* disappeared from view but, with pounding heart, his private admirer saw, reflected in the glass of the doors, his departing form with its unmistakeable rocking walk. There followed the reflection of the double rank of surplices, like a swarm of white butterflies, then the guttering candles and finally the priests' green vestments. The singing moved round behind, as the choir turned back up the south Choir aisle, but the man's gaze was still fixed on the glass doors, as though he could somehow conjure the procession up again, making it run backwards in absurd fashion, like a trick film. The boy had looked at him, had purposely sought him out, as if he knew and understood the effect his gaze would have.

*I know nothing whatever about you and yet, in that brief converse of glances, I already know everything about you, your hopes and desires, all expressed to me in that special language which is ours alone. There is a secret and peculiar bond of trust between us, and you, young man, began it all...*

When he reached the Close, he noticed that the cloud-bank had broken, leaving only a few white wisps against the blue. He got into his car and drove away, trying to come soberly to terms with what had just been happening. But, the further he went, the more aware he was of being still inside the Minster's sphere of influence, as though caught in some vast invisible net, - and at the heart of the sensation was a spot of light, of warmth, like the sun shining on a surplice, or on a boy's pale face.

There were a few very rare people whose sexuality went before them, filling a great space as would a sweetly scented herb. The senior boys would soon be going through that process which would deepen their voices, put hair on their bodies and temper the fresh eagerness of their childhood, while inciting guilty feelings, as had happened to him at that age. In most of them, the phenomenon would go largely unremarked by the insensitive outside world, but in the case of one man and one boy the beauty of this progression stood a chance of being, at least privately, signalled, recognised and appreciated. Whatever rules he had made and broken in the course of his life, there were two which were steadfastly observed: never to be bored, and always to accept situations which were clearly ordained from outside.

*

'What's up, Morri? You OK? You're a bit queer today. Well, all right, not *poofy*. You know what I mean.' His opposite number was trying to jolly him on, as they sat in school over hot chocolate and biscuits, in the short pause before Matins.

'Just shut up, Filly, will you? I need to think, that's all.' Despite the sharpness, he was in a strange state of elation, as never before, as though he'd been presented with a fabulous new toy which he neither could nor would share with another. He was torn between an urgent need to talk to someone else about it, and the knowledge (for, even at thirteen, he was no fool) that it would be dangerous to do so.

'Ah, good,' said Dr Hutley, the sub-organist, from nearby. 'Fig roll. I like fig roll!' The timbre of his voice and the nuance of naughtiness carefully built into such utterances had left generations of boys in no doubt as to the man's true propensities. Hutters was someone you were careful not to find yourself alone in the organ loft with. Christ! That man up in the *Dec* stalls, what did *he* sound like? If it was anything like that, he'd be a right turn-off!

Fillingham had sidled up again, clearly anxious to impart some great piece of information. 'Have you heard? Whittie's made it to big game, and he's going to do us a demo tonight.'

'Count me out, I'm busy,' was the curt response from the boy, who had much more important ideas in his head than another's coming-out ceremony, even though it was regarded among the seniors as bad form to miss one. He had grown beyond such smuttiness, he was now on a serious fishing trip, whose prize was somebody the others might very well envy him for, if only they knew.

*

Just before noon, he turned into the driveway of the cottage. The sun had firmly established itself, a breeze was blowing, and the smell of the sea hit him as he wandered through the gardens and paddock, across the dunes and down to the beach. The sand was firm and perfect, the glittering water washing over it in small, foamy waves leaving a salt spume behind. Apart from a large tanker on the horizon, there was no sign of life.

Nearly six months ago, a chance assignment (which he had been within inches of turning down) had brought him back to England, to a frozen cathedral town in the east. Used to a comfortable and elegant life abroad, he had been shocked to find that accommodation suited to his needs was simply not to be had in Wharnley, the choice being between expensive but indifferent hotels and squalid furnished flats.

In the end, he took two fairly decent furnished rooms with a landlady who was out working most of the day, and reluctantly moved in, intending it to be just a temporary base in the town, a postal address for convenience. As soon as the winter began to yield, he started looking at properties to let in the undulating country beyond, and almost immediately found, and fell in love with, "Stella Maris", a large cottage standing alone on the coast, some two hundred yards from the sea, and protected from the wind by some gnarled, leaning trees. Undoubtedly his painterly eye had something to do with his choice. Although he had spent little of his life near the sea, it always exercised a fascination on him.

The place was an even longer drive from his work than was Wharnley, but he took a six-month lease on it without hesitation. 'In fact, it's on the market,' the agent told him. 'The owner's gone to work in an embassy abroad. You would get it for a good price, sir, if you were interested. It does need one or two things doing to it…'

How right he was! Having once been two dwellings, the building was long and narrow, the middle now occupied by the staircase and hall, leaving a largish wing on each side, one of which contained a large lounge, the other a drab kitchen, dining-room and store-rooms. There had once been four bedrooms upstairs, until the present or past owners introduced what the agent's printed description called "some civilising touches", by pulling internal walls about to create new bathrooms, (so English!) Outside, they had even put in an asphalt drive-way up to a new garage. Nothing had been properly finished off, however. As it was empty, he brought over some of his own furniture, and purchased some more. If he *were* to buy the place, he could make a more personal mark on it, later on, though it would require a monumental act of faith on his part, not to mention the expense.

He had never thought to bring anyone else here. Indeed, at this time in his life, there was no-one whom he would wish to bring. There were no close friends and, since Mother's death, no relatives. He had stashed one or two memories away in the lumber room, but had no desire to stir up the dust that covered the boxes of photographs and letters, those self-inflicted punishments which he always felt bound to bring along to places he inhabited, however briefly. Curiously, they offered him some small feeling of security.

Rambling along by the water's edge, he watched the waves obliterate his footprints, leaping backwards whenever one threatened to come up over his shoes. Inside, he was as ruffled as this sea, and the wind buffeting him in the face was like the effect on him of a boy's gaze. He stopped, looked along the rippling line that tenuously divided water from land, and saw a figure slowly coming towards him, head lowered. Reaching him, the boy looked up, a serious expression in his eyes. 'What do you want with me?'

'What should I want with you?'

'Then why do you look at me like that, in the Minster?'

The trouble was that he knew and yet did not wish to know, was afraid of letting the old genie out of the lamp again, of daring to contemplate tasting what Thomas Mann called "the infinite delights of depravity", with all their perils of physicality.

He could magic up the boy's words, but not the sound of his voice. Barry's had been deep and firm, Jonathan's fluting and affected, betraying at once what he was. He sometimes heard them at night, Barry's 'It's no use,' over and over again, Jonathan's querulous 'Roland, come here. I want to speak to you.' And Mother's dying look, which said: 'I understand how it is with you, son. We are what we are, and no-one can change that.' Barry spoke of desperation, Jonathan of jealousy, but Mother radiated only comfort and tolerance. And Fiona? One ought to remember the voice of one's wife, even after eight years of separation, but it had gone, leaving only one phrase: 'A bi-sexual is a traitor to both causes.' She saw her mission as saving him from himself, which brought a tinge of bitterness whenever he thought of it. Not even she could have achieved the impossible.

'What should I want with you?'

A wave caught him unawares, filling a shoe. He walked back through the dunes, unlocked the door into the dining-room, went through to the kitchen, took a piece of steak from the fridge and turned on the infra-red grill.

It wouldn't do, it couldn't possibly work, however many situations his mind might conjure up, however many exchanges with *him*. The cottage offered an escape from all kinds of things but, most especially, from a boy under whose spell he seemed about to fall.

It was a waste to be cooking for one. Barry, Jonathan, Fiona and Mother were gone, scattered to the wind, four scars of *amertume* on his heart, four gaps left in his life.

He prodded the steak, looked at the vegetables simmering, took out cutlery and a plate, and tested the temperature of the wine in the fridge. No, this was a vacuum he did not choose to fill, not in the same way – not even to combat the dead feeling of *ennui* which so often afflicted him these days. He was not prepared to run the risk of another heartbreak. There was a layer of moisture on the outside of the bottle, like that thick dust on the carvings above the wooden stalls in the Minster. Ice protects, insulates…

He found a prayer book and turned to the psalm they had sung as they went out. *"I will take no wicked thing in hand; I hate the sins of unfaithfulness; I will not know a wicked person."* Did that boy understand the things he was made to sing?

He switched on the transistor radio on the sideboard in the dining-room, but before he could find the French station he usually listened to, treble voices rang out as if in mockery, and he turned it off again. The steak was almost ready. He poured out some wine and took a sip. The coldness bit into his palate, made a nerve jump in one of his teeth. He suddenly felt out of sorts, without any appetite, because his weakness of will had risen up to taunt him, to accuse a man who one minute was poised to make the decision that would return him to sanity, only to find it swept aside seconds later by a shaft of sunlight and the look in a boy's eyes… This would not be the first time in his life that he had fallen victim to his own irrationality. For was he not one of those creatures put on this earth to learn everything the hard way?

\*

During the next week he paid two visits to his place of work where, since November, the project had claimed most of his time and energies. Site visits in a hard hat were a new thing to a man who spent most of his time as a designer and artist, working at home. He did not even need this job, but the planning and supervision of the interior redecoration of a large fire-damaged mansion, (so different from drawing sets and costumes for operas), had caught his imagination. And besides, he had promised Mother, just before she died, that he would return to England now and then.

His career had flourished so well that he had made a name for himself. Inevitably, he had got to know all kinds of people, but on a purely superficial level. Only three people had ever succeeded in making any inroad into the complex series of barriers and defensive works which he had thrown up about himself, but these deeper relationships had always gone wrong, leaving him soured and scarred. Not that he had sought to become a recluse, but it was clear, from an early age, that he and society went their own separate ways and that, to survive, he had to manage some dissimulation.

They had known, of course: Fiona and Mother, probably even more than Barry and Jonathan, had known about the façade and what lay behind. They had discovered those things in him which he was ever reluctant to admit to, and he had always been amazed that they accepted him, up to a point, more readily than he accepted himself.

Prey to any number of disturbing thoughts and memories, he forced himself, during the rest of the week, to work in the garden, weeding, digging, sawing branches, - any welcome distraction which offered itself. For amusement, he spent some time planning how he would alter the place, were he to buy it. There was over an acre of land, much of it covered with semi-derelict orchard and vegetable plots. He would keep the fruit trees which tailed imperceptibly into the woodland to one side of the building, but the vegetable gardens would most probably be turned over to flowers, and a terrace built. Behind this, the sizeable paddock was encroached upon at its outer edge by the dunes, so that the boundary fence on the seaward side was almost silted over at one point, making it very easy to pass through, to get access to the beach. One might plant a number of fairly mature rhododendrons and conifers along here, to act as a wind-shield. How very different from his gardenless flat in Switzerland!

The interior would also require some work done on it, and this gave him serious doubts about acquiring the place. If the smarmy house agent thought he had a sale already, he might be in for a disappointment.

When, on the Saturday, he lay in late, he was able to see it in perspective at last, this business with the boy. Whatever the latter's opinion about it might be (and it was wiser to avoid creating any more imaginary conversations on this point), the man knew his own mind: he would resolutely stay away from the Minster this Sunday, returning on the following one. If the chorister ignored him, he would know that the contact was either broken, or had existed only in his foolish brain. If there *was* an acknowledgement, it would be sensible to take no notice. Either way, one would be cured simply by the passage of time, by a fortnight passed without their seeing one another again.

Sunday came, he walked over to the village to pick up some newspapers, but could not concentrate on them. Whenever he closed his eyes, he was back in his stall in the Minster. He took up the service card for the umpteenth time. They would be there at this very moment, singing the Eucharist, and *his* gaze would be roaming about, looking, wondering…

He hurried out through the gardens and paddock towards the wild tumble of sand dunes which seemed to mock at his tidy work in the garden. The wind blew into his face, tossing his hair about, his feet stumbled in the sand. The sea lay boiling and foaming beneath a leaden sky, the cold, dull sand stretched far away in both directions, without a soul in sight. As if in a vision, he became detached from himself, observing events from another dimension.

He saw a man throw off his clothes and let the gusts buffet playfully at his nakedness. Planted like a Greek statue on the shore, proud, defiant and beautiful, he stood with one foot slightly in front of the other, on which his weight was balanced, one hand on his hip, the other dangling at his side. The head was tilted up, fair hair fluttering in the breeze. The sea rushed up over the sand, touched his foot and receded, as if guilty of disrespect to a god. But the playfulness of the scene was wasted upon this grave figure: eyes flashing, the chest heaving and falling, he collapsed upon the beach, weeping, rocking to and fro, beating great hollows in the wet sand with his hands. His body, just now a divine and beautiful whole, was but a collection of contorted limbs without dignity, the eyes broken, the mouth trembling and uttering unintelligible sounds of defeat.

*

The last touches were being put to the Nunc Dimittis just before the service, and the Director of Music was in a temper. The boy had spent most of the practice staring out of the window and down the road which, bordered by a high stone wall, ran along the south side of the Minster. Cars were already drawing up, their occupants getting out, smoothing themselves down, mutating into that most traditional and respectable of bodies, the congregation for Evensong. But where was *that man*, who had been so conspicuously absent from the Eucharist this morning? Mr Baines all but spat at him for muffing an entry, Hutters hit a chord on the piano, and the section had to be sung all over again.

As he sang, he suddenly saw the blue Mercedes, (left-hand drive), come crawling along, looking for a space, and felt his heart quicken. It was all right: his foreign friend hadn't gone away at all. He sang his heart out like an angel, and got a grudging 'That was a bit better' from the Director, before they all trooped off down the spiral staircase to the choir vestries, to get robed up.

*

Evensong was early on a Sunday, and the clock was striking the half-hour as he crossed the patch of green outside the vast, grimy west front. Medieval kings, once victorious in battle, looked down on him in pity, pigeons fluttered about and, somewhere above his head, a soft bell began to ring.

Hurrying through to his customary stall, he noted on the way that very few people were present. Good, the boy would not fail to see him. But no – he would surely have forgotten the stranger, busying himself with far more interesting matters than a man who sometimes appeared at a service. It was mere wishful thinking to suppose anything else. The half bottle of wine he had drunk with his lunch was turning to acid inside him.

'What should I want with you?' Your youth, your innocence and *beauty?* Was that too much to ask for? He knelt down, his wilful mind trying without success to frame a prayer. They were coming in already, and he got to his feet just in time to see *him* go past, for whose sake alone he was here, but too late to know if his presence had been registered. His heart was beating savagely. He did not know at which point in the day he had broken his resolve to stay away. All he knew was that he was now standing opposite the chorister – *his* chorister - , all scruple hurled to the winds, and willing him to look up and across.

*And he did.* As the choir turned inwards, the dark-haired boy's eyes swept quickly along his row, purposefully, seeking. Their gazes connected, and he gave the slightest of nods, as if to say 'Ah yes, there you are again. I hoped that you would be.' The man stood there, full of thanks and jubilation. *So it matters to him whether I come or not.* Perhaps he had even felt some small regret this morning, to find his furtive idolater absent.

The priest was speaking of the mystery and majesty of Christ's ride to Jerusalem. Of course, Palm Sunday, the beginning of the crescendo that ended with Easter. Spring was about to become summer, and the very notion produced a new sensation within the man, as if his inner reserve had begun to thaw, allaying all the moral doubts which recently had been plaguing him. For, in this matter, he was definitely not on his own any more. They sang a long psalm, but the man stood with his prayer book as though transfixed, not taking his eyes off the boy for more than a few seconds at a time. The music was evidently new to the smaller boys, for the bigger ones shared their books with them and pointed, like teachers, to the page. *He* was next to a very tiny boy, one of those whose heads scarcely came above the ledge on which the music was placed. The observer was affected by this obvious concern for his charge, and the little one looked up with the kind of respect very occasionally reserved for an elder brother. This could not however compete with the blaze of attention which the older boy was receiving from the man opposite.

The interminable psalm came to an end, to the apparent relief of the boys. He even saw his one wink and smile across at his opposite number, as they sat for the lesson. At first he was charmed by this good humour and, when their eyes met again during the reading, there must have been an answering twinkle in his own. But then his elation turned to ice: was this boy just playing with him, using for his own amusement what for the man had become an intense and serious exchange? Perhaps he had told the others about it at night, when the talk in the dormitory turned to the comic, the sinister and the forbidden. Were these nods and winks some kind of signal to announce the presence of an adult whose behaviour was highly intriguing? 'Watch him, and you'll see. He does it all the time.' Sweat broke out on the man's brow. A fond fool could all too easily be made to look ridiculous.

As though the anguish was showing in his face, he saw the boy looking back at him with that grave, level gaze, and his heart was immediately calmed. 'I won't give you away, don't worry,' was the message in that look, making him feel ashamed to have trusted the boy (*his* boy) so little.

He was now consumed by the desperate need to be here: it was no longer enough to come once or twice a week for the private communion with him. He would gladly leave the cottage for a while, move back into his rooms in town and so be well placed to descend more regularly into the arena.

Had he not dared to put this boy on a pedestal, admiring him perforce from afar, as Gustav von Aschenbach had done with *his* boy? The vital difference was that this was Wharnley, not Venice, and, now that the contact seemed to be established on both sides, he was curious to know this choirboy's name, (for to know a person's name is partly to possess him), and somehow find out what *his* thoughts were about this unconventional relationship, if it was not too fragile a thing to be called that. Of course there would be problems: they were not two adults, between whom the striking up of a casual conversation was so easy, with all the possibilities of taking things further. A man and a choirboy, whatever would the world say to that? If Aschenbach had passed through Tadzio's doorway, how would the critics have reacted? He found himself trembling at the very thought.

Just now, while the choir was singing the anthem, he noticed that when the boy sang high notes he raised his eyebrows, as if straining to reach the top of the treble range. It could not be long before his voice would start to break. Not a boy any more, but a young man. There were so many imponderables here, so many obstacles in the way, however innocent their future path might prove to be. And yet, he was not prepared to give up the struggle so easily. It was, after all, anathema to an artist to ignore inspiration, in whatever form it came – and he was nothing if not true to his art.

\*

The iron tongues sounded the Westminster chimes high above the school where, after all had gone quiet, a gaggle of the older boys had collected in a dormitory to witness Whitwell's new-found skills at self-production. Only one senior was absent from the ritual: closeted in his room, (for the black-cloaked choristers enjoyed a privacy denied to the rest), he sat listening to the remorseless bell-notes, and speculating where a certain person might be at that moment, and what doing.

He took out his father's letter again. His parents tended to write only when something displeased them, and this conveyed, in no uncertain terms, their deep disappointment at his poor academic record during the past months. *"You have a perfectly good brain. When do you propose to start using it?"* It seemed as if he'd always been used to reproaches instead of encouragement. If only he had an ally, a proper friend to talk things over with, he might feel more like using his brain! This stranger looked as though he might be understanding and sympathetic, but how to get through to him? That was the problem.

Never before had he felt like this about another person, nor been in such a state of anticipation. He only knew that all special relationships began with the eyes, and that he was now embarked upon something wickedly outrageous, though it was very serious too, and not just a game. If the man with the Mercedes was truly interested, and he looked as if he was, then it was time to find an opening, a way of moving it on to the next stage. After all, life was all about learning new things, wasn't it?

\*

The following morning, while he was doing some work in his rooms in town, something – the increasing heat, perhaps – made him open the window. At once, above the noise of the traffic outside, he heard a bell, far away and high up: the Minster clock, striking the hour, a summons which he could not deny, however busy he might be. The hope of maybe seeing *him* was bound to be frustrated, for he would surely be at his lessons in the Choir School.

Meeting a verger in the nave, he was flattered to be recognised and greeted. As though drawn by the same unseen power which had acted on him that very first afternoon – changing him irrevocably, it seemed – he passed beyond the huge transept and entered the south Choir aisle where the sunshine made bars of light on the ancient pavement. Through the open door of the choir vestry, the long rows of cassocks and surplices were hanging up, waiting for the next onrush of choirboy mice. His eye was immediately attracted to the four black capes on their hooks. One of them was surely *his* and, there being no stewards or vergers about here, no priests to come prying and ask what he might be doing, he slipped into the vestry and, like a spy gathering illicit intelligence, fumbled with the first cape till his fingers found the label stitched inside: "M. Whaley". The next bore "J. Cove", the next "P. Moriston", and finally there was "K. Fillingham". He did not need to write them down, for they were already etched into his memory. But which was *his?*

Avoiding a large guided party, he crossed the Choir before the high altar and went through into the little north-eastern transept. Here, two ancient doors, linked by a passage, led through to the cloister, where the hot, brilliant sunlight beat down on the square of green turf sown with tomb-lids. In a remote corner were Saxon stone coffins, unearthed during excavations. No tourists had as yet penetrated this far, and so he was surprised to find his thoughts interrupted by a sudden flurry of movement, a few yards away, at the chapter-house door.

At first he could not believe his eyes: boys, dressed in white shorts and singlets, short white socks and plimsolls, were coming in a great throng out of the chapter-house, each carrying a chair. He moved to one side as they streamed by, turning the corner and disappearing through the doorway beneath the library which connected with their school. He realised that these were all the boys, not just the choristers, and he also knew exactly what was about to happen.

Would the choirboys recognise a man, pinned here against the wall, his restless mind reciting the litany of the four names over and over again? No, they were laughing and talking among themselves, evidently in the best of spirits: white forms flitting past, voices echoing along the arcade of pillars and wooden vault. Pink, bare arms and legs, young bodies dressed for sport.

*He* came almost at the end, slowly, carrying his chair as if it were something fragile and precious. Appalled and yet triumphant at his daring, his admirer took a deep breath and turned slightly to face him, aware that Fate, having kept them hitherto at a distance, was now throwing them together. His boy was tall and it was apparent, now that he was not wrapped up in his robes, that he was fairly slender in build, though quite muscular for his age, with a springiness like that of a young animal. His shoulders were quite broad, his back was straight, his hips narrow, his buttocks full and well-formed, and the backs of his smooth white legs a delight. Good thighs gave way to developing calf muscles, and the dimple behnd the knee was still soft, dark and secret. *Who are you, then? Is it Fillingham, or Whaley, Cove or Moriston?* A priest brought up the rear, hurrying along the laggards with 'Come on, or we shall never be ready in time. It's their sports day,' he added to another man and woman who had just come into the cloister.

The boy approached, his gaze fixed on the uneven stones over which he walked. As he drew level he looked up, checked his movement a little, as if in surprise, then let his dark eyes look straight into the man's, with the suspicion of a flush rising in his cheeks. His expression was serious, as always, understanding and polite: he looked, but did not stare, he responded, but did not make his admirer feel the need to avert his own gaze. Indeed, the man stared openly after him, watching his every step as far as the corner, where he passed out of sight, re-appearing tantalisingly for brief moments between tracery and columns. Then he was gone, and the end of the strange procession with him. The priest banged the door shut, and the spectacle was over.

The man fled away in confusion to where the stone coffins stood in a severe row, and sat down on the hard cold corner of one of them. He had never properly conceived of the boy as a physical being until this moment, never thought that this soul which seemed to commune with him could be enclosed in a body so utterly charming. True, his features, his hands, his movements had been attractive from the very first moment, but never had his admirer imagined him laid bare like this, where white-clad innocence was beginning to yield to the growth of early adolescence. If he had been delighted by this boy before, he was quite stricken with a painful joy now and, perched uncomfortably on the coffin-lid where the dust of death still lay, he whispered the ancient dangerous words of life, of youth and of longing: 'I love you.'

*

*"Dear Father and Mother, I'm sorry my last report wasn't better. I'm sure you will be more pleased with the next one, as I have now started to work really hard. Even my teachers have begun to praise me!"*

Instead of letting out the true reason why things had so improved, he padded out his letter with snippets about the last cricket match (and the score of runs he'd made), which would definitely appeal to Father. There were certain recent developments in his life which he knew would be like dynamite if he included them here, so he stuck to neutral topics. They wouldn't understand about the other things, anyway. And this letter, if it was like the last few, would be slow to reach them.

If any other man were to look at him like that, he'd take him for a sick pervert, but this was different. As soon as he caught sight of the man in the cloisters today (how did he know to be there, just then?) he wanted to be *seen* by him, as an ordinary boy in gym kit, instead of togged up for a service. When their eyes met, he felt an electric charge go through his body, even though neither of them spoke. If only they'd managed to say something to one another...

A feeling of angry impatience came over him: for the first time, they'd been so close, they could have spoken – if Byatt-Woods and the others hadn't been around. All the man needed to do was make a proper meeting, somewhere safe for both of them...

*

At the Staff Meeting, some boys' names were being raised in discussion.

'His Maths is coming on in leaps and bounds, at last,' said Mr Thorpe, an earnest young man, who was also the boy's tutor.

'He's actually managed to read a whole book by himself, without my having to hold a gun to his head,' said Miss Speight, with a kind of acid admiration in her tone. She had absolutely no illusions about the boys entrusted to her for English lessons.

'Used to be a real wet lettuce with his singing,' said Mr Baines. 'I nearly demoted him, you know.'

Someone else said, 'Why the abrupt change? Is he in love, or something?'

This caused a titter, and a frown from Canon Byatt-Woods.

'I'd like to put in a word about his French,' said Mrs Dowd. 'And only the other day he said he'd like to take up German when he gets to his next school.' She did not add that, when she pressed the boy to give a reason, he had gone pink. Sensitive child, that one, with the makings of a fair linguist.

'Latin?' The Deputy was always anxious to know how the boys performed in Classics.

Mrs Dowd gave him a vigorous nod.

The Headmaster, who had noted down a few comments, now added one of his own: 'He's not a dunce, for sure. I think we might feel more able to recommend him to try for a scholarship. Where do you suggest, Alec?'

Canon Byatt-Woods was not only the Deputy Head, but also the power behind the throne. He had contacts in most of the public schools, and used them to advantage. 'Let me see now… We've told Fillingham to go for Sallowburn and Cove for Oundle. I don't think we should point this one towards anywhere too prestigious. He might go off the boil again, which wouldn't do our future prospects with them any good. I suggest Keatwells. They're always after good musicians.'

'Ought we to contact his parents, do you think?' the Head wanted to know.

'They leave these things to us,' said Byatt-Woods somewhat brusquely.

'Where are they, again?'

'Greece, Turkey, I know not,' said his Deputy with a shrug. 'Father's an archaeologist working for UNICEF, and his wife assists him, as I understand it.'

'It bothers me that he doesn't seem to have any friends here,' ventured Mr Thorpe.

'Yes, I've noticed that,' said Miss Speight, who had made a study of social bonding in schools. 'He's one of the most self-contained boys I have ever met.'

Outside, the Minster clock began to chime. The Head looked rapidly round his Staff and said 'O-kay. Point number nine. Repairs to showers…'

*

He had always regarded freedom of action to be his most cherished possession, resisting the attempts of the world to commit him to its ways. At times when others were being swept past in the main stream, he would be sitting alone on the shore, watching *their* destinies playing out, never his own. He refused to be tied to another's will, even in the very few relationships which he formed. Others might regard that as vanity or arrogance or selfishness, but he saw it merely as a defensive stance. He had never wanted the trammels of the world upon him, had always taken the solitary's path and, when that path crossed another, the meeting had generally been joyless and unfulfilled. Barry. Jonathan. Fiona.

His experiences at school had marked him for life: five years to be suppressed, expunged from his memory. To comfort himself against the rigours of its unyielding routine, he had become briefly involved with another – the only source of consolation in those dark days. They had parted company at eighteen, and he had never seen him again. The effects of all this had been reasonably contained until now, but they had come back to the surface with an alacrity as frightening as it was exhilarating. For him, the metaphorical image of the mirror was not of a glass for Narcissus to admire himself in, but of something to turn one's face away from, for fear of what one might see…

Now, since the moment that he had discovered a young boy sitting opposite who, by his mere existence, had thrust a mirror into the hand of a man in the congregation, he had begun to detect some changes in himself, which, till now, would have been out of the question: the uncommitted one was becoming committed, willingly leaving his precious freedom outside the Minster door, for the sake of a tacit converse of eyes, for the fleeting moments of a new and fanciful madness. (For that was surely what it was). He had allowed himself to become chained to the very place he had struggled to break away from, compelled, like an uneasy spirit, to haunt its aisles and sanctuary, hoping for he knew not what, but ever returning, ever driven on by a compulsion to sound the depths of this new experience.

It was certainly not the first time he had found himself in love, but he knew about the perils to be faced if one dared to overlay mere boyishness with adult yearnings. Turning over in his heart all that had so far happened – tenuous though it might seem – between the boy and himself, he knew that he was too immersed in it to be able to extricate himself now. What might have been a safe and possible option, a few days earlier, had had a solid shutter banged down in front of it, leaving him naked and vulnerable. And what effect might it be having on the object of his affections?

The afternoon stillness of the great building was reluctantly giving way to the echoing shuffle of people's feet, as the vergers asked the visitors and tourists to leave, causing a slow mass retreat out of the side chapels, the east transepts and the Choir – a westward surge, leaving a vacuum to be filled by the few souls already in the stalls for Wednesday's Evensong, and by clergy and choir.

With a boldness worthy of Aschenbach himself, he stood beneath the arcading of the south Choir aisle, not far from the vestries. The sun, as he could see even from here, was streaming through the western windows of the lantern tower and picking out the gothic pinnacles of the organ case, perched like some absurd wooden castle above the stone screen.

'Will you be staying for the service, sir?' This was precisely how it had begun. He made some excuse to linger on for a few more minutes, and the verger smiled and withdrew, as though he had divined the man's true purpose.

At the same moment, he heard a door bang over on the north side, the tramp of feet approaching, and his pulse quickened. They were coming with rapid boys' steps along the north Choir aisle, and they would soon round the corner behind the high altar reredos and pass by him. In panic, he thought of retreating into the chantry behind him, to spy unseen on the one he loved, but invisibility was in fact the last thing he wanted.

They came in twos, led by the same clergyman he had seen in the cloisters, twenty boys in dark-blue blazers, the little ones in grey shorts, the older ones in long trousers. His boy was at the front, next to the fair one. Then came eight pairs of smaller ones, with the other two seniors bringing up the rear. Feet clattered over the paving as they wheeled past.

His heart was in his mouth. After yesterday's encounter in the cloisters, it was a matter of life and death to him to capture *his* gaze. And he was not disappointed. The boy's grey eyes gave him a quick sidelong glance, unsmiling, almost furtive, like the gesture of one who does not wish to be caught out. As always, the man returned the look, the blood pounding at his temples. Now they were gone, disappeared into the choir vestry to get changed, while the organ's soft, deep notes explored their way round the delicate tracery and carvings, echoing back from the high vault, before dying away in the vastnesses of the long nave.

With incisive voice a solo reed took command over the other stops, and sketched a theme: the first line of a hymn. Time to move, if he was to take up his usual position. The music swelled as though in welcome, he hurried up the steps and through the arch into the Choir, occupied his usual seat and knelt.

A loud and martial motif overlaid with a trumpet fanfare now swept the congregation to its feet, as though the organist was proclaiming a special act of rejoicing for his benefit. The choir processed in, hymn books were opened, papers rustled. The man stared across, his fingers working aimlessly through the prayer book, and the boy looked up, as if a spark were dancing between them, so powerful and blinding that their surroundings disappeared momentarily into darkness, and the organ notes seemed muffled beyond the thumping of his heart.

In a second it was past, and a priest was leading the General Confession, but his lips refused to take part in what was for him more like a straitjacket than an offer of spiritual renewal. He was not penitent for something that in his eyes was beautiful, not wrong. The boy whom he loved, who knelt opposite now, possessed a radiance and freshness which delighted him. If this was God's doing, then the sin lay in ignoring God's work.

Blissfully, he let the music of psalms and canticles wash over him, his gaze discreetly brushing that of the boy whenever they stood up or knelt down or, more daringly, during the lessons and sermon. His mind played a child's chanting game: Fillingham, Whaley, Moriston, Cove. He even craned to look at the other cloaked choristers, trying to match names to heads of blond hair, dark hair…

At the end, as his boy marched out with the rest, the man sank to his knees once more, the names whirling through his brain like a stupid tune which refused to be stilled. The organ postlude pursued its course, the handful of other people drifted out, a verger came in to extinguish the candles on the lectern, and then a chorister (one of the smaller ones, back in his uniform) appeared and began to collect up the music from the stalls.

When the boy reached the men's stall immediately in front of the man, he leant over and said, in a low but insistent voice, 'Tell me, what's the name of the tall dark-haired boy who sings over there, on the end?' And, with a hand that was not quite under control, he pointed across to his boy's empty place.

The little boy stopped gathering booklets and looked up at his questioner. 'That's Moriston, sir.'

He felt like a man half-way to a triumph. 'And his first name?'

The boy hesitated, but did not take his eyes off him.

'Is it Peter?'

There was an odd expression on the child's face by now, and he had reddened a little. 'Generally,' he stammered, 'we don't use first names at school, but he's called Piers, actually.'

Piers Moriston. *I receive the name as if it were a talisman to protect me from all harm.* 'Has he gone back over to school yet, do you know?'

'He was still in the vestry talking to Mr Baines when I came in here, sir. Shall I go and see?'

'No thank you. That's all.'

Wondering whether he should have found some way of swearing the obliging child to silence, the man crossed the Choir and left it again by the passage leading to the cloister. Piers Moriston. The closing notes of the organ voluntary died away and he counted the seconds of echo, as if to do so were a magic charm that would bring his boy to him. Piers…

Loitering outside the little chapel by the cloister door, he stared up at the mural with four bishops, high above his head. Their faces, though faded and discoloured with age, seemed to look down with compassion, reminding him of the kindly chaplain who, years ago, had prepared him for Confirmation. As the classes drew to an end, he had called his charges into his study, one by one, but instead of the Catechism the talk was of darker things: the spilling of seed, and the wrath of God upon idle hands that did the Devil's work. Much adolescent blushing, embarrassed priest in book-lined room, its leaded windows overlooking an English garden in high summer. This is where the guilt had begun. Puberty was a sin to be brought before

God: promises made, broken, made again and broken again, an eternal cycle of remorse and relapse, to underline the weakness of one's humanity.

Footsteps were returning from behind the high altar, and he steeled himself to remain where he was, almost in their very path, where *his* boy, Piers, could not fail to see him, alone and waiting for him. This time, the priest was not with them, and they came back in a more leisurely way in twos and threes, chattering quietly to one another. He stood there awkwardly, his hands at his sides, his spirit apparently bent on pushing his body into a difficult and conspicuous position, the one rebelling against the other. But reason was scattered to the winds. He was prepared to let things take their course, whatever it may be, and, like Faust summoning the Earth Spirit, thrust on "though it should cost me my life."

Piers came on his own, behind all the others, to all appearances dawdling and studying a piece of paper. The door into the cloister banged again, the others were gone, and only he was left, approaching with his rocking walk. Blue blazer, coat of arms on the badge. Smooth brown hair with a fringe falling to just above the eyes. Mouth open. A picture of fresh innocence to make one ashamed.

His admirer knew all too well the views of the present-day world: infatuation for a boy of thirteen was ridiculous, degrading for a man and, if he knew of it, incomprehensible to a boy. Such things just did not happen, modern society was not like that of Ancient Greece, where such love was once prized. Instead, it went to great lengths to protect its children, safeguard their loveliness and beauty until these had passed into something deeper, more mature. Outsiders with thoughts like his had no part to play in their upbringing and, if an illicit contact should be made and subsequently discovered, there was Hell to pay for the offender. How many people felt such a forbidden affection for a child and yet were compelled to repress their feelings and act out a charade of respectability and obedience to the law? He could not continue any further along this path, something he should have realised when he returned here last Sunday: it would and could never be any use.

The passage was not very wide and, since he was planted near the door, Piers practically had to brush past him. Knotted up in his anguish and embarrassment, the man could not help taking a last look at that dear face, whose boyish features were illuminated on one side by the wan light from the east windows of the little chapel. He was pale as a cherub on a monument – young, but already bearing the suggestions of later maturity.

He looked up from his paper and his eyes met those of his admirer, whose expression must have been registering a mixture of surprise, pleasure and shock, then gave a quick, shy half-smile, even opened his mouth to frame a silent 'Hullo', and checked his movement a little. It looked for all the world as if he was going to stop for a chat, but then someone came back through the door, said 'Come on, Morri!' in a stage whisper, and the boy blushed scarlet and, with a flash of anger in his face, slipped away into the cloisters. It was the big fair-haired boy who had come to disturb them at that holiest and most pregnant of moments.

The man turned away in dismay, needing yet again to find a quiet corner in which to be alone with his thoughts, but already a group of visitors was invading from the north aisle, forcing him to return to the Choir. Sinking down into a stall, he put his head in his hands, as though in prayer. That smile had brought him literally to his knees, had irredeemably shattered his new intention of a second before. It had been so sweet, pure, spontaneous and communicative, that he could not have said more with words. 'I know what you are feeling for me, and I don't mind at all.' And that angry look showed him that Piers was as frustrated as he, that their possible and so needful meeting had been thwarted. The obstacle only further hardened his resolve.

*

As soon as he reached school, he went straight up to his room, shut the door and sat down on his bed in glorious amazement that a grown-up should want to come and find him like that. He knew it, but did not, hoped but dared not believe in it, he was swept away on a wave, not caring when it would break on the beach. He might be just a lad still, but what was happening inside him made him feel much older. He could leave the other boys to their silly dirty little tricks. He was growing up, growing towards a man who, he was now convinced, was out there waiting to speak to him. If only bloody Filly hadn't ruined it, at that moment… He looked at his watch – no time to be lost! Grabbing his cap, he dashed out in search of Squires.

*

As the man walked out, still bemused, the sunlight blazed down at him, matching the unaccustomed jubilation in his heart. Throngs of people were strolling about by the west front or pouring through the gate into the little square with its tourist shops. The delightful balm of early summer lay over everything, the world was turned to gold as he followed the crowds through the dark gateway and so beyond to where the castle projected its yellow turrets out of the greenery, with people like lookouts on the topmost pinnacle. A motor coach was picking up passengers, a teeming mass of colourful movement amidst the ancient buildings lining the square. Now and again, a blazer could be seen.

The coach roared away in a thick cloud of exhaust; pigeons flew lazily through the air. He idled along towards the gift-shop just beyond the gateway, where four or five people stood looking at the trinkets, post-cards, guides and souvenir spoons on display. Two boys in dark-blue uniform with caps were there too, causing him to stop abruptly in his tracks. A large American in dark glasses bumped into him from behind and swore, but he took no notice, for his eyes were riveted on the taller of the boys, looking so conventionally schoolboyish there, amid the window-shopping adults, that he could hardly believe that it was the same. The other boy (the little one who just now had been tidying up the books) was saying something and pointing in the window. Piers murmured a reply, but his pursuer was just too far away to catch even the sound of the voice above the bustle in the square. He found himself clenching his fists, breathing hard and willing the other child away out of sight, so that his boy would be there alone. He could have destroyed the Temple at that moment, so taut was he, so desperate for success.

For a moment he closed his eyes, and immediately the air went cool, a breeze blew about his head, and when he opened them again a small cloud had passed in front of the sun, the square was gloomy, with pieces of paper blowing about in its dusty corners. The tourists had all gone, but outside the gift-shop stood one solitary boy in school uniform. The man walked slowly over, stopped beside him and pretended to look in the window also, feeling all the while like one who, faced with two seemingly identical roads, the first leading to life and the second to death, has to make a choice without knowing until afterwards which he has chosen. The air felt chill now, the contents of the shop window were in shadow, and he was shivering.

The boy made no attempt to move away. The man could have put out a hand and touched him on the shoulder. So much had his intentions changed, in the minutes since their last encounter, that his mind was still dazed, and he had no tactic prepared, no plan of action whatsoever.

As he turned his head towards the boy, Piers looked calmly back with an expression that seemed to say, 'We're away from the Minster at last, so what are you going to do now?'

The man managed a gruff 'Hallo', the schoolboy touched his cap automatically, then looked as if he wished he could take it off and hurl it into the gutter.

'They let you boys out, then?' He was painfully conscious of his awkwardness, the assumed avuncular tone. It was all wrong, and yet this was how it must start. The boy was looking disappointed, he felt. Didn't he realise that one must play a slow game, go patiently through all the steps?

'Yes sir, for three-quarters of an hour.' He was surprised to hear the man speaking in a perfectly ordinary English accent, and found himself having to take great breaths, like a fish coming up for air.

His voice is lower in timbre than the shrill treble of the little ones, with just a trace of Scots in it, but what really attracts me is the note of *involvement* I believe I detect here, giving me the opening and confidence which I so sorely need. 'So, then, might one ask what you do in your three-quarters of an hour?' (Play it by the rules, but remember that every phrase spoken does not bear just its face value).

He shrugs. 'Wander around. Do some shopping. It's good to get out.' And, as he says this, he is studying my face.

My mind begins to function logically at last. Perhaps my impression was right: the boy really is tired of the incessant round of singing, practices and lessons, lonely even. I take a firmer grip on the reins: 'Is an admirer of the choir permitted to invite one of its senior boys out to tea?' Surely he'll realise that this humorous tone is false? In me there is a deep ferocity of feeling now, burning up any lightness of touch, and the seriousness of it is both image and reflection of the sweet gravity in my boy's face, when he looks across at me in the Choir. If we could only thrust aside these games of deceit, souls might meet and speak a plain language. *An admirer of the choir.* I am mistaken if I believe that I have become rational: I am trapped in a web of crossed lines, where my words, like hunks of rough-hewn wood, do not begin to convey my true thoughts.

The sun returns, its heat filling the square. And the boy Piers, whose face at first registered slight surprise at my question, smiles, a real smile this time, straight in my face and nothing shifty about it. The eyes soften, and there is mischief playing in the corners of his mouth.

'Of course, why not? Thank you very much, sir.'

I choose a dim corner in the little beamed tea-shop round the corner and order tea. Useless at producing small-talk to order, I perpetrate the stupid blunder of asking him his name.

He looks back at me, and there is sheer devilment in his eyes now. 'But you know already. That kid, Squires, I was with just now, said you'd asked him.' There is a hint of victory in his voice, and I know that I am well and truly caught out. There is no answer to this, unless it be the whole truth, and we are not ready for that yet.

But Piers – bless him! – does not let this put him off. To him my gaucheness is probably far less important than our success in making contact at last. 'It's really all right, sir. I just hope he gave you the right name. He can be a bit of a practical joker, that one.'

'He said you are Piers Moriston.' I hear my voice uttering the words like a spell, as if I really possess part of my boy at last.

He nods, a trifle bashfully.

'Piers… That's a name I like.'

His half-smile vanishes. 'I don't, but I suppose nobody likes their own name really, do they? And what about you, sir?'

This was usually the moment I dreaded, stepping out into the public arena to introduce myself. Now, though, it comes tripping off my tongue with an ease that astonishes me.

He immediately repeats my name aloud, and I had never before thought it could sound so well. 'I know what *you* do for a living, Piers, but I'm an artist and designer.' Another flash of amusement in his face, rapidly stifled by the demands of etiquette.

'What's wrong?' I know it must sound stupid, brusque even, but my inspiration of a moment before has deserted me. To have him so close to, and to see his face so animated by my answers, fills me with sweet bewilderment.

'Sorry,' he is saying. 'You see, I'd somehow got it into my head that you must be German, or something.'

'*German?* Now what could possibly have made you think that?' I egg him on now, conscious of matching his mischief.

He leans forward, his eyes bright and conspiratorial. 'Saw you getting out of your car one day. Merc, isn't it? German number plate? It's got "GE" on it.'

'Swiss actually. Geneva. But in fact I'm really just as English as you are!'

'I'm half Scottish,' he begins, but, doubtless feeling that this sounds cheeky, stops in some confusion. 'Silly of me to get your number plate wrong.'

I was realising by now that, although our first proper contact was loosening a little with every step, we still had to invent a common language if we were to make any progress. It was a matter of some relief that so far Piers seemed so incurious about us. Perhaps a sense of protocol stopped him from asking me tricky questions, such as '*Why do you keep looking at me and following me?*' It was one thing to have a conversation of eyes, with all that that implied, but a very different affair to begin verbalising one's actions. At present, he seemed content to leave the initiative to me, but how much did he really understand the implications of all this? Or I, come to that?

To keep us on safe ground, I continue to deal in platitudes. 'Do you board, Piers?'

'Yes, all of us in the choir do. Most of the others are day-boys.' Still polite, but he does not take his eyes off me. I now recognise, in his frank, open look, a hint that he is ready to cut the preliminaries short, should I offer him some kind of opening.

The tea arrives, making a welcome diversion. All too aware of my own foreign awkwardness in this most English of situations, I offer him a scone, pour two cups of tea and then pass the milk and bowl of sugar lumps. Only then does it occur to me that tea is probably the last thing boys of his age would choose to drink!

'It's really very kind of you, sir…'

'You don't have to call me that, if you don't want to,' I say gently. 'I'm not one of your schoolmasters.'

Piers flushes scarlet. 'Sorry. I didn't mean to. That is, we've always been told we must be polite to - '

To strangers. Great blocks of formality, like ice-floes, still keep us apart. I adopt a new tack. 'Where are your parents, Piers?' Even as I say it, it occurs to me that he might think I am prying, but he obviously does not mind.

'Somewhere out in Turkey at the moment, uncovering frescoes in old churches, as far as I know. Don't hear from them all that often.' His embarrassment shows. 'Well, they do send a postcard now and then, and they remember my birthday. And I sometimes get a rather critical letter.'

I look at him. He is clearly flummoxed at having spoken so frankly to a stranger, but it only warms me to him even further. I never was a parent, but if this boy were my son, and I had to live at a distance from him, I would write him only letters of love and encouragement. 'May I ask how old you are?'

'Twelve years and ten months, to the day.'

'You're big for nearly thirteen.'

He smiles, and a look of pride comes into his face. 'I'm in the sixth form at school.'

'And what do you do in the holidays? Go to Turkey?' It matters a great deal to me to find out all I can about him, so tenuous and brief is this meeting. What I have, I hold...

'It depends...' As he carefully lowers his cup, I notice again his beautiful fingers, and the dæmon in my mind is urging me to tell him how handsome he is, despite knowing the risk of dire penalties awaiting those who cut corners in this game. Besides, if it is true that beauty is in the eye of the beholder alone, he might be confused or even scornful.

'I stay with a relative mostly. Sometimes I meet Mother and Father abroad, and once in a while they come back home. We've got a flat in Hertfordshire, but it hardly ever has anyone living in it. They're very free. I mean, they let me choose more or less who I want to stay with, if it's not them.'

His words send an arrow of fond hope coursing through me. 'What are you... planning to do this Easter?' The initiative rests with me, and I am certain that he would go with me to the cottage, if I invited him.

But he pulls a face. 'I'm going to spend the hols with this aunt. Family tradition. It's pretty awful. Well, you see, she's getting ancient now, but she likes me to go. Her son died when he was about my age.'

Pausing before putting a piece of cake in his mouth, he quickly adds, 'But it's not for long, thank goodness. I couldn't stand that!'

And then, at the very moment when it looks as if we have exhausted all the possible small talk, and might be ready to move on to something momentous, he glances at his watch. 'I'm afraid I must go now.' At least he does not call me "Sir", this time.

Taking care to hide my despondency, I wish him a happy Easter, and he gets up rather stiffly. 'We must have tea again together after the holiday, Piers. That is, if you'd care to.'

He smiles and says, with a delightful stammer, 'I really would like that. I've enjoyed talking to you, very much.'

Before I realise what I am doing, I give him my professional card, bearing the address of my rented rooms. 'My phone number's there. Give me a ring when you get back, will you? I shall expect a full report on all your doings!'

I keep it bright and businesslike, but I notice that same expression in his grey eyes which is always there now, when our glances meet during services: the spark of tacit understanding, reassurance and even affection.

'Of course I'll do that, Mr Millan. I promise.'

'And I shall be at the services, as usual.'

'Right. Oh, there's no sung service tomorrow or Good Friday. We're back on Saturday, though, and the Sunday Eucharist of course. The Bishop comes to that one! Anyway... thanks very much for the tea.'

In an instant he is gone, but he leaves behind such a warm after-glow that I could laugh aloud. Piers, Piers. I am giddy, incredulous, still in sweet ignorance of the role I have begun to adopt with you, and you with me.

I pour the last of the tea into my cup, then watch my trembling hand choose an iced cake, place it on my plate and cut it into a ridiculously large number of minute pieces. My mind is struggling to prepare a balance sheet of dignities and indignities. On the plus side, I have met Piers Moriston face to face and finally talked to him, as I had never in my life talked to a boy of his age. Our words might have been of little consequence, but then we had already forged deeper links, from the very first moment our eyes met at that Evensong, centuries ago. We had become like conspirators, thieves in the night, we had begun, without discussing it, to dismantle the barriers that divide the younger from the older, the man from the boy. We had even begun to set up some unspoken ground rules, the embryonic beginnings of a language of affection and trust.

On the minus side, I had raced ahead too fast, and probably dragged him along with me. My interrogation of the boy Squires had not gone unnoticed nor unreported. What else was common knowledge to the boys in the choir? How discreet was Piers, whom I had made *my boy,* as though he had somehow become my property to command? I had planted myself in his very path, stared across at him in services with unaccustomed boldness. *Who else had witnessed that?*

I had to concede that I did not really care: what happened between Piers and me could be of no significance to the rest of the world. We had been brought together by something outside and above ourselves. It was better to accept the fact, and move on from there. I was comforted to know that he had opened this exchange, he had sought me out in the first instance, and not the other way round. The last thing I wanted was to be responsible for him, especially as he had just given me every indication that he had the situation well in hand.

One thing made me smile: if I had been fishing to find out his name, *he* had been keeping watch for *me*, had discovered my car, even taking me for a foreigner! We were in the power of that delicate chemistry which either unites souls or severs them. He evidently approved of me, his deference towards me being tinged with a delightful freshness and confidentiality. He did not, and could not, know of my deeper feelings for him, and it was right that it remain so, at least for the foreseeable future.

Sleep deserted me totally that night. I kept getting out of bed, going to the window and staring uselessly into the darkness that cloaked the Minster up on the hill where, nearby, my boy, my Piers, would be slumbering like an innocent. We had stormed a set of defences today, perhaps even taken some irrevocable steps, and all during a pleasant half-hour or so in which I had sat at a table and drunk tea with the boy whom, in an astonishingly brief period of time, I had come to treasure more than anyone else in the world.

As if doubting the reality of what had just happened between us, I went over all our encounters and today's exchanges in my mind: there were those delicious visions of him walking into the Choir in his black hooded cloak, or, like Tadzio, in his white shorts, carrying a chair through the cloisters, or (surprisingly young-looking) in his blazer outside the gift-shop.

Was I allowing Mann's story to colour my views, and attaching too much importance to it all, or were Piers and I really embarked on a voyage together? My wayward sense of wish-fulfilment gave me a vision of a ship which had set a definite course, would come through the fortnight's flat calm ahead of us, and then strike boldly out to the great ocean. "If all the world were dead, and only we two left alone…"

Piers, I believe I have already taken a step beyond Gustav von Aschenbach, who merely loitered outside the door of his Tadzio. I have tried the handle of that door and, finding it yield to me, am ready now to enter a place holier than any sanctuary. I, hitherto free, have run my colours up the mast in your presence. Surely you must see my fondness for you, however haltingly expressed. And I dare to believe that my feelings are, in some measure at least, reciprocated!

I was ever prone to leap right into the centre, scorning the cautious, conventional path trodden by other men. Once I saw my way clear, I would push ahead, heedless of the outcome, for the greatest crime in my book was to be bored.

*

He could think of nothing else, he scarcely touched the supper in the boarding-house and, when he rushed off upstairs, it was to sit on his bed in a feverish glow, turning over and over in his mind every word that they had said to each other, and taking the card out of his pocket a dozen times, as if to prove it hadn't been a dream.

His greatest concern was that Mr Millan, having seen him from so close to, in the very ordinary setting of a café, would think him just a weed, lose interest and abandon him. Their talk had, after all, stuck to normal things. His own feelings were strangely mixed. Oh, he liked Mr Millan even better than before (though he'd been surprised to find he wasn't a German at all), but he couldn't work out what might happen next.

He sounds a very decent sort of man, but he went out of his way to inquire about my name, and he took me out to tea. He seems to be all on his own, he isn't like a parent or any other relative, come to that. More like a friend, even if he is so much older. A very special kind of friend…

I'll write to him, here and now, and send it to the address on the card. It'll be a bit like fan-mail. Will he mind? It was the most difficult letter he had ever written in his life.

*

The Choir was fragrant with the heady smell of flowers, candles and, today, incense. The organ voluntary grew to a triumph of improvisation on the Easter Alleluia, trumpets and reeds stabbing out, the stalls vibrating beneath the surging sound. I knelt, my hands resting on the oaken shelf in front of me, and tried to frame a request for grace and comfort in the time ahead, as though the festival could bring me no joy today. I had woken with a qualm in my heart: suppose Piers too had thought over our conversation, seen the ill-concealed interest and eagerness in my face, and, with the coolness of hindsight, got frightened off? Would he have divined those things in me which were not for his ears and eyes, at this early stage? Would he even grant me a look across the great expanse of the busy Choir today?

Reflection of candles in the glass doors beneath the organ screen, as we got to our feet, a shaft of sunlight on the silver processional cross, white butterflies flitting in lines: all the old excitement was there. I rose to watch him as he headed the choir in among the throng of people, the Easter Anthem echoing to the vault in a glory of praise and redemption. The sun beaming down from the clerestory on the south side picked out the carved pillars, the rich dark wood of the ancient choir stalls, the boys' fresh faces and the glitter and magnificence of the vestments of the approaching bishop and clergy, so that I, quite overwhelmed by the splendour of it, could not utter a note.

The choir had taken up their positions, and the last verse was dying away, before I dared to look at him. He stood there as always with head tilted down, eyes looking out under their brows, mouth open, hands fidgeting: Piers, to whom I had spoken at last, who had been touched by my kindness, and who had promised to meet me again. I stared at that dear face, willing my eyes to carry the imprint of its features for a whole fortnight.

We knelt. Looking across the heads of the basses immediately in front, I caught him peering at me through the gap between the shelf and the supporting rail, as if he knew what was seething inside me, and I was thankful that, after all my (and maybe his) misgivings, my boy still wanted me.

They sang the Kyrie, men's and boys' voices alternating and finally blending together in a union of harmony exquisite to the ear. When, after the Collect and the Gospels, everyone faced towards the altar, and the plain-chant of the Creed mingled with the incense smoke, I could see the pale purity of his cheek and neck. What would be going through his mind? When we turned inwards again, he looked at me and actually smiled. Piers, Piers, this is dangerous play! You can get away with a nod or a wink at one of the boys on the *Decani* side, but a signal away over their heads to a man standing in one of the alcoves – a man who is always there, and who returns your glances... We must be careful: people don't understand when something is harmless, they construct all kinds of jealous and sinister fantasies. Who is that man? They might ask. What is he to you? Why does he look at you like that, lie in wait for you, and why do you smile at him, take tea with him, *flirt with him?*

Although it pained me to do so, I lowered my eyes, refusing to answer that smile, half ashamed to seem to be on the side of the wall-builders, of those who would think it an affront to the dignity of the service if people noticed me exchanging private tokens of affection with him.

One thing I now knew for certain: I would no longer be content just for us to meet on rare occasions in the tea-shop. A quieter rendezvous was called for, away from public gaze: a secluded and special place where we could simply be ourselves, free from all this secretiveness, taboo and inhibition. Piers' fresh youth and beauty gave me hope, for in his innocence he might fling between us that rare bridge of mutual love and understanding which had so far eluded me. He might even go with me to "Stella Maris"!

The bishop ended his sermon, the priests moved about like colourful chessmen on the carpeted pavement, and the congregation rose for the Offertory hymn. Prepared to pay highly for the privilege of standing opposite my special boy, I took a note from my wallet and deposited it on the plate, a paltry price to give for so much light, life and love. Men have built cathedrals for less.

Again we knelt for the long progression of prayer leading to the Communion itself. When the moment came for everyone to leave their seats, I looked up to see Piers rise and go off to the altar with the other older ones. I so much wanted to follow, to kneel beside him, but, while the organ played quietly and the priests performed their slow ballet in the sunbeams at the altar rails, I saw the one whom I loved take Communion far off, as if in another world.

Then the congregation began to file out and form up in two lines, the choir were returning and I timed my exit so that I would be sure to pass him. It was over in a second, and I had to be content with a quick sidelong glance, which he answered. My legs were weak as I joined the line on the right, making me fearful of possibly causing a commotion by fainting at the altar steps. I felt so exposed out here in the arena, expecting a verger to draw me aside, warn me about unseemly behaviour and exclude me, by order of the clergy, from taking Communion, lest I should increase my own damnation. The looks between us would surely have been noted, triggering a secret system to defend boyhood innocence against a predator in their midst.

There is a buzzing in my ears, my eyes lock on to a panel of painted glass in the great east window, where Adam and Eve stand naked and simpering, the pinkness of their flesh mingling with the foliage. The overpowering smell of incense is like a drug. Even as I stare at the couple, strange things begin to move and rustle around them, peeping out of the trees and bushes of Eden – horned creatures, grotesque beings taking up lewd postures – and the buzzing turns to cackling, hooting and shrieks of immoderate laughter. My head spins, I see myself running over to Piers, fighting to tear off his black cloak, loosen his tie, rip open the buttons of his shirt to reveal his pink torso. Already, in my mind's eye, he is one of Donatello's singing *putti*, with chubby little arms and animal expression and, as I rend the last garment, he is naked before me, with laughter in his face, a jeer, and an invitation…

A tug at my elbow, and the steward was showing me to a place at the altar rail. The vision had rapidly passed, but my body was drenched in sweat as I received the bread and wine, still trembling with terror and delight at the profane scene I had witnessed, my lips pressed to the Cup where *his* had just been. I still did not understand what was happening.

The choir was singing the Communion hymn and when I drew level with Piers, his voice, like the cooing of a dove, detached itself for a fraction of a second from the others and projected its own timbre and beauty across my path, while I sought out my stall, sinking down like a man in a trance, quite at a loss to know how to cope with all this.

Shortly after, the priests having completed their business, we sang the Gloria, and a Blessing was given by the bishop. The music grew from a few soft notes to a strident blare that was quite unwelcome to my befuddled mind. As the choir began to process out,

Piers gave me a last slow look, which cut me to the quick. When he had passed from my sight, the organ fell silent and the mingled voices of the departing men and boys took up the psalm: *"O praise God in his holiness."* The chanting moved round behind me, as they passed from the Crossing into the Choir aisle, but I could still see him in my mind's eye, long after the reflection of the butterfly surplices had vanished, to give place to the bishop and clergy in their pomp and glory.

The psalm died away, the people knelt for the last time amid the aroma of incense and extinguished candles still hanging in the air, then a distant muttered prayer came from the vestries, the Dean uttered a curt 'Thank you, gentlemen', and that was all. Nothing remained for me but to traverse the length of the nave in sorrow. As I passed into the west porch, the inner door clanged shut behind me, and the echo rang back, as if in mockery, from the dark tower vault.

*

> *The Choir School,*
> *Priestgate,*
> *Wharnley.*
> *Maundy Thursday.*

*Dear Mr Millan,*
> *Thank you very much for the tea yesterday. There was so much I meant to ask you, but time ran out. You said you were an admirer of the choir but (I hope this isn't too bigheaded) you really seem to mean me! I wanted to say anyway that I'm really pleased we have met and talked. It's hard to write all this down, but I'll drop you another line from my aunt's place. I expect I'll have a lot of time on my hands!*
> *Thank you again for kindly taking an interest in me,*
> *Yours very sincerely, P Moriston.*

There was also a P.S. to the effect that he hoped this letter would get to me, "because of the Bank Holiday". It was delivered on the Tuesday after Easter, and my hand shook as I read it. The artless child had not written between the lines, he had come straight out with it. Could it really be that he wanted to get closer?

As always, when there was an emotional burden to shoulder, I threw myself into my work, driving even on the Bank Holiday to the burnt-out mansion, where cherub faces in the smoky plaster reminded me always and only of Piers. Somewhere in the restored design I would include my boy's face – and my own – in the manner that carvers of ceiling bosses in cathedrals put, for the sake of immortality, a self-portrait, or even a pet mouse…

\*

It was raining, and he had refused to go out with his aunt Mavis to walk the dog. She had grumbled at him, but he had dug his heels in, and she had stomped off in disgust. She was usually quite decent to him, but today she'd been on at him again about leaving water on the bathroom cork floor. To hear her, you'd think she was a pinched old spinster quite unused to the phenomenon of a boy in the house who, like any of his ilk, could be messy, untidy and gloomy all at the same time. He'd been tempted to retort that he didn't believe in being mildly irritating when, with a little more effort, he could be bloody infuriating but, seeing the set of her chin, decided not to push his luck too far. She'd already threatened to turn him out, to camp on soggy Meriden Green!

Yesterday she'd been affable enough to pull his leg, when he'd been sunk in stupor, thinking about Mr Millan (who was always "Roland" in his most private thoughts now). He spent a lot of time trying to work out what it was about the man that he found so attractive, and ended up by deciding that, if the magnetic appeal was right, anyone in the world could be drawn to anyone else. It suddenly seemed so simple.

And there had been that dream, with Roland in it, which gave him no rest. He did not stop to ask himself about the normality of having a man so constantly in his mind: the idea was there, it would not leave him in peace (not that he wanted it to). A man had chosen him – no, they had chosen each other, from the very first moment they were in the Minster together – and the thing just seemed to gel without their needing to sit round a table and work out the whys and wherefores of it. Other people, if they knew, just would not understand it, but there was no need to involve them. Exactly as in his dream, there were the two of them, and that was sufficient.

*

'What's the matter with you this time?' demanded his Aunt Mavis. 'You're even more do-lally than usual. You wouldn't be someone's starcrossed lover, by any chance?' She was a keen supporter of Shakespeare, and always going to his plays.

He'd smiled what he fondly hoped was an enigmatic smile, and she'd laid into him, goodnaturedly enough. 'Seriously, it's not another boy, is it?'

He'd blushed, but assured her that it wasn't another boy.

'Who then?'

He merely answered 'Ah!' and she capitulated. 'Well, whoever or whatever it is, you seem to be mostly happy and – what's the modern jargon word? – adjusted. Are you happy and adjusted?'

He thanked her and said he'd never been more so, and she offered to write and tell his parents about this 'enormous improvement' in him.

Today, in his gloom, the idea of writing a letter suddenly appealed, like a cure for homesickness. He got a piece of her nice letter paper, found a ball-pen that worked, and sat down at her desk.

> *21Burnsill Close,*
> *Meriden*

*Dear Mr Millan,*

> *I hope you are enjoying these weeks more than I am. Life in the dead centre of England is just that – dead. I've been into Brum with my aunt, but didn't like it much. It's very noisy and dirty and there are some rum looking people around, such as we don't get in Wharnley! Which reminds me to stop writing about myself and ask how you are.*

> *I hope it's not inconvenient if I scribble to you. I'm not much of a letter-writer, but it helps to pass the time, and it's always good to get one from someone else!*

> *Very best wishes,*
> *Yours, Piers (Moriston).*

*P.S. We may be going to Stratford tomorrow.*

*

I sat on a wooden seat up in the park with a book in my hand. Beyond a high stone wall, the towers of the Minster floated among small white clouds speckling the blue. The park was heavy and fragrant, its great trees swollen with foliage, through which a stiff breeze was blowing. I was making no headway at all with the English translation of Mann's story, and since Piers' last letter arrived I had felt useless and helpless, shuttling like a lost soul between my rooms, my work-place and the cottage. At first it hadn't been too bad: my memory of him remained fresh but, like a flower, it faded all too soon, and I had no proper picture of him. Depression overcame me, with the irrational feeling that I might die before I saw him again.

One day, climbing the steep lane up to the Minster, I had to stop and let the pain ease from my chest. The towers thrust upwards, far above me in the trees, like the crown of some great and inaccessible palace. It was very hot, my limbs ached, and, half-way up the hill, I had to abandon it and turn back, because I had simply lost the battle. Even at thirty-five I was too old for Piers, I should have realised with good grace that I was no longer a match for any such youthfulness. As I stood gasping on the slope, a youth ran swiftly up the hill past me, like a young deer, as if to scorn my weakness.

The period of deprivation passed slowly, and despite the joy of having received two letters from him, I began to believe that my worst fears would be realised after all. At night, I lay awake for hours, wondering if I might sometimes be in his thoughts, as he was all the time in mine. I had imaginary conversations with him, and was once granted a dream in which he appeared, though nothing to rival that wicked and delicious vision at the altar steps. I was sitting in the nave of the Minster among many other people, waiting. As in a fresco by an Italian master, the vaulted roof was a dull green colour, and the various stages of the lantern tower above the Crossing receded into blue obscurity. Somewhere in front, in the distance, a boy's treble floated, unaccompanied – his voice, ethereal, incorporeal and utterly haunting. Then it stopped, and I saw a figure come running towards me through the arch in the screen, black cloak flying out behind. He stopped by me, looking at me, and touched me lightly. I put both my hands on his shoulders, bent over and kissed him on the forehead, only to wake and, with acute misery, face the grey daylight seeping into the room, as if to punish my unruly sleep.

\*

'Where is it to be then, after Wharnley?' she asked.

'I'm trying for a music schol at Keatwells.'

'And where's Keatwells, when it's at home?'

'Dorset. I want to start German there, if I can.'

His aunt snorted. 'Why German, for goodness sake? They destroyed poor old Coventry, you know.'

He had it on the tip of his tongue to tell her about Roland, and that he'd once believed him to be a German, which was where the idea to study it came from. It had sort of got into his blood stream. Instead he said, 'It's a useful one to do with French, and it'll help me to get a better job, later on.'

'Don't you want to follow your pa and ma into archaeology?' There was a twinkle in her eye.

'Not likely! I'm not spending the rest of my life in the desert, with stones and bones. I've had enough of all that, working in the Minster!'

\*

> *"My dear Piers,*
>
> *It was so nice to get your letters. Life here has been rather quiet. I'm sure that the Midlands must have attractions for a musical young man like you. Didn't Mendelssohn put on the first performance of 'Elijah' in Birmingham? A bit before either of us came on the scene, admittedly! And Stratford is a charming old town, even if packed with Americans, who all seem to think they own a stake in it.*
>
> *I trust the rest of your holiday will be pleasant, and I look forward to hearing from you in person when you get back here. You have my phone number.*
> > *Kind regards,*
> > *Roland Millan."*

As I reread it, my heart sank: the tone was so safe, so avuncular, (in case his aunt should get hold of it and start drawing unwelcome conclusions). Despite the pallid style, would he get the real message behind it, the loneliness, the longing, the dreadful chasm inside me which had opened up on Easter Sunday and refused to close again, as long as the two of us were apart? It was quite incongruous, maybe, but like my hero Aschenbach I recognised the pain as something beautiful in its way, and not without honour.

After spending another ten minutes agonising what to do for the best, I crumpled up the letter and threw it in the bin. I dared not let him have anything by which I might be identified. As it was, I had given him my card. Idiot man! So, Piers, the ball is now back in your court.

## *II.*

There was a strange but powerful paradox in it: as my sense of loneliness and frustration grew, so did my creative powers. My opera designs, which I thought had reached an *impasse*, took fire again, and innumerable drawings of Tadzio flowed from my pen, in sailor suit, in town clothes, in a turn-of-the-century bathing costume – every head bearing the dark fringe and intense eyes of the boy I loved. One day, for rare relaxation, I devoted a lot of time and care to a pencil drawing of choirboys in robes walking outside the Minster, portraying them all as mice. I had it framed in the art shop at the foot of the hill, resolving to give it to Piers later on.

When I calculated that he must have returned, I remained in my rooms, taking all my meals there, waiting for the phone in the hall to ring. I was curiously out-of-sorts, my body a mass of stupid aches, which kept moving around, rendering a visit to a local doctor quite pointless.

'Are you under any particular stress?' he wanted to know, as he tapped at my abdomen, telling me to breathe deeply. I decided to keep my problem, inasmuch as I understood it, to myself. It might too easily appear like a bad case of unrequited affection.

A magazine editor, for whom I had done a lot of work, rang me from Paris, but so afraid was I of missing Piers' call, so sensitive were my emotions to the smallest setback, that I headed her off after a sentence or two. In a few days, I managed to alienate most of the few people I was in professional contact with, and wondered if I might be going out of my mind.

The summer term had become two days old, dark-blue blazers had made their unmistakeable appearance in the streets, and still Piers had not phoned. I relapsed into melancholy, avoiding the Minster at all costs because I was afraid of looking a fool, and anxious not to offend against protocol, knowing that I had no choice but to wait until he was pleased to receive me. The awful doubt grew like a cancer: he had found friends during his holiday and forgotten his admirer, or worse: he had not forgotten me, but thought it wiser to have nothing more to do with me. Perhaps he had blurted it all out to his aunt, and received a stark warning for his pains. I cursed myself for not having leant upon him to get out of his duty visit, and to go with me instead. I could never hate him, but I hated myself for my cowardly weakness.

Tired of waiting for the phone to ring, I drove up to the park, where I could at least sit and dream in the knowledge that Piers was not far away. Eyes closed, I leaned against the wall, which was warm and comforting to my back. The smell of ancient mortar together with the scent of herbs and sweet flowers was in the air and, for a moment or two, my cares lifted.

As if through the eyes of one of the four painted bishops, I looked down on a man standing in the north-east transept. Though the cut of the neat plain grey suit was not English, this was no tourist. He was caught in the wan light filtering in from the window of the side chapel: a fair-haired man, thinning a little on top, but still quite striking, with large, mobile lips and dark shadows round hazel eyes. A rather Germanic face, a handsome face, all the more so for its sad expression. A face to look at, to peep at from the other side of the Choir, a face to fall in love with, perhaps. With a gesture of doubt or timidity, he put one hand to his mouth, and three rings, worn for self-reminder, self-punishment, not love, gleamed in the dim light. One from Barry, one from Jonathan and one from Fiona. Three unions contracted over the space of seven years, and all of them destined to fail. Now he stood there, contemplating what?

It had been a gloomy grey morning when they let Barry out, wearing his crumpled suit and clutching an old case. He got in the car and I gave him a packet of cigarettes. We were both embarrassed and awkward. Barry lit up straight away, but wouldn't look at me for a long time. We had already discussed what lay ahead between us, planned for this day, looked forward to it with joy, as one greets the end of winter, - but the winter would not yield. I understood that he would be nervous and insecure at first, that he couldn't leave it all behind just because a door had clanged shut. Freedom had to be savoured slowly, like rich food after a long period of starvation. I glanced at him from time to time, where he sat hunched up, with a vacant expression, and my warmth froze to disappointment. I wanted Barry, and was glad to have him, but he looked all wrong here, outside. He fitted into a cell – it seemed to be his destiny. He'd been in three times, after all, and the outside world terrified him, as he admitted, when he finally spoke. I told him not to be  frightened – I would look after him.

'You don't understand, do you? I'm just bloody scared of being tempted, that's all, because I've got no fight left.'

We set up house together, and he got a job. Printer, on a newspaper. We sealed our bond with exchanged rings and a party for some friends. It managed to last thirteen months before Barry was whisked off inside again, and I was left with the ruins of failure. I should have moved us away from London, away from a randy sixteen-year-old lad in the print shop, who regarded him as fair game from the start. Which he was.

I believed, though never actually knew, that Barry was cut up by his infidelity to me. I visited him only once after that. His face was grey, he shared a cell with a man twice his age and a kid of nineteen, and it was quite clear what the set-up was. It was a relief, in the end, when he begged me not to come back. I wrote once or twice, but never received a reply. Like pouring water into the sand...

A small plane was circling overhead, and I opened my eyes for a second to the blinding blueness above me. As I twisted round, searching the sky, there was the roof of the Choir, where men were working, replacing sheets of lead. They could have been angels, poised in stone on the roof-peak, looking down upon the solitary man below.

I looked at my hand. Next to Barry's gold ring was a slim platinum one. Jonathan and I discovered each other while viewing a museum in Athens, where rows of statues, the glory of Hellenic male beauty, were preserved in a calm coolness remote from the nearby heat of sun on ancient stone. He was short, dark, and already quite fat. We were the only people in the gallery, and he turned his gaze on me and said, in not very good Greek: 'What beauty! Almost too much beauty!'

'One is rather overwhelmed by it,' I replied in English, and thereby sealed my fate. His eyes lit up, he swaggered over to me, exuding odours of perfume and sweat in equal quantities. The signs were unmistakeable.

'Surely one cannot have too much?' To this day I do not know why I went with him. As a lover he was clumsy and impossibly possessive. I suppose I took pity on him, for his loneliness matched my own, and there was always the chance that a new relationship might wipe out the painful memories of its predecessor. He adored me from the start, even to the point of finding in me the kind of beauty we had admired in the statues. Before we knew what was happening, we were embarked on what was intended to be a mutually revelatory tour of the world. I soon discovered the reason for Jonathan's selfishness: he was impossibly spoilt. Heir to a flourishing cosmetic firm, his task in life was not to work but to wait until the fruits of other people's labours dropped into his lap.

To be continually idolised is bad for one's ego and sense of proportion, and in some ways it was just as well for me that the break came after our journeying together had lasted a mere six weeks. We were in Florida, preparatory to going on to Mexico, and already quarrelling over the type of hotel to stay in (nothing being too good for him, whereas I, who had to earn my living, insisted on a fair amount of economy), the exact course of our itinerary (he had a horror of air travel) and, worst of all, the type of people we mixed with.

The latter was the cause of the final fiasco one evening. I have always tried to put on a gregarious front when in company, to give my lopsided character a veneer of stability, whereas Jonathan was very much a one-man person. Very early in our relationship, he made the cardinal error of thinking he owned me. While he was upstairs, finishing dressing for dinner (an elaborate process which took him an hour or more), I happened to strike up a conversation in the lounge with an American girl whom I had already noticed on our arrival. She was a few years younger than I, attractive, and so clued up about Europe that we were engaged in animated talk on a settee when Jonathan eventually made his entrance. When he caught sight of us together, disgust was written large in his face, and he came to a halt just inside the doorway. I beckoned to him to join us, but he remained where he was, evidently searching for a suitable insult.

The American girl was looking up in surprise, when Jonathan burst out with 'Roland, come here. I want to say something to you,' so loudly that the other guests turned to look. Acutely embarrassed, I motioned to him again but, because he was stubbornly standing his ground, I shook my head and tried to continue talking to the girl as if nothing had happened, all the time aware of the darkly dramatic figure over by the door. I had only got a few words out when he screamed, in a rage, 'If you don't come here this instant, Roland, I shall shoot myself.'

The atmosphere was charged like a Chekhov play. Faces stared at both of us in disbelief. Enraged now, myself, I waved him away, assuming this to be another piece of bluff. He went very pale, as though something within him had been punctured, and then slunk away. If I had known that he kept a loaded gun and was capable of carrying out such a threat, I would have run after him and perhaps be chained to him still. One shot finished our relationship with almost welcome neatness. Fortunately, he was a bad aim, and only made a mess of his shoulder, but there was consternation in the hotel. Sylvia kindly kept me company until my now ex-friend was out of hospital and on his way back home, solo. The world tour was mercifully over.

And what was I doing here now, alone in this remote English cathedral town, devoting my time and attention to a choirboy of all people? *Was this not some kind of madness?*

The man who had been standing by the cloister door looked restless and nervous and, at the approaching footsteps, seemed ready even to turn and run. But then came the slamming of a door, reverberating for several seconds far down the nave and stopping him in his tracks. Nineteen boys passed by, and still he waited there, calmer now, and with an expectant look. An angel descended from somewhere above and came slowly past him, dark-haired boy with milky skin and large dark eyes, a half-smile playing at the open mouth, a quick look from beneath the delicately curving brows. And the man rushed away to hide his confusion.

He was not the first one to have hung his flag in the wind, waiting to see in which direction it would blow. Tadzio on the beach, Piers outside the gift-shop in the square, alone, waiting and ready for the call.

*Ready for the call!* I opened my eyes and leapt up from the bench with a suddenness that made the blood rush to my head, blinding me for a few moments. I was ready for the call, and he wanted me, would be trying to contact me even now. Of that I was sure.

Even as I opened the front door, I heard the phone ringing in the hall. Dropping the key, I picked up the receiver. The pay-tone sounded at the other end, then there was a second's gap and I heard a boy's voice say: 'Can I speak to Mr Millan, please?' I sat down on the floor, striving to control the joy in my voice.

'Hullo, Piers.'

'Oh, hullo.' He sounded diffident, and I made myself get the conversation going. 'You're back, then?' (Silly question!)

'Yes, sorry I didn't get through before, but...' The voice stalled, then picked up again. 'Did you get my letters?'

'Yes, thanks very much. You remembered my invitation to tea?'

'Well, yes. Actually, I've just had some money come through. May I invite you, this time?'

'I'd be absolutely delighted, Piers. You name the place and the time, and I'll be there.'

This was salvation after all, come to hoist me out of my loneliness and misery. 'I love you, Piers,' I said, a fraction after I had put down the receiver. If I had said it to him directly, would it have frightened him off?

*

Soft clatter of cups, sunlight blinking on spoons and knives. A gentle murmur of conversation penetrates to our corner. Piers' eyes are bright today, matching my private excitement.

'Why didn't you phone before?' The opening greetings over, I can no longer restrain my impatience, though I try to make it sound surprised and humorous.

He is embarrassed, I can see. 'I was in sick bay for a bit, as soon as I got back. Tummy bug, probably from my aunt's insanitary kitchen. And then...'

'And then?' I cannot resist a gentle prompt.

'Oh well, you know, I didn't want to appear - ' his voice tails off, but I know exactly what he means: *I didn't want to appear too forward.*

Not wishing to make things rush ahead in this seemly English setting, I force myself to ask him to elaborate on what he reported in his last letter, but he merely wrinkles his nose. 'She's very kind, really, but she just isn't geared up to someone my age. I think four days would have been about bearable, but two weeks...'

The tea arrives, providing us with a few moments' diversion.

'Are you going to, Piers. It *is* your treat.'

With a slender hand he lifts the tea-pot, pours a little into a cup, stops and raises the lid. 'I think it needs a stir.'

I help him out by putting milk into the cups.

Piers carefully drops four lumps into mine, pours the tea, slowly hands it over, and looks at me seriously, as if he were performing a sacramental act.

'You have a remarkably good memory!' We had joked about my greed for sugar the last time. As I pick up my cup, our hands brush. His is soft, smooth and cool.

'For some things.' He says this with more than just a touch of emphasis and then, with one more apprehensive little glance at me, he stops pussyfooting and out it comes: 'I had a dream about you while I was away.'

Piers, this is no mere boyish avowal, no casual comment, but one charged with an adolescent intensity! I think my own face must be registering something like exhilaration, for there is an answering glow in your eyes that goes well beyond the steady look you have so often given me in the Minster. There's even anxiety in your face, because you don't know how I'm going to react to that!

Now that we are sitting so close, it is quite clear that my involvement and preoccupation with this boy are not one-sided: he sees, he understands and responds, and I feel a geat responsibility for the one sitting opposite, who pours me tea and who dreams about me. Just as I dreamed about you, night and day, Piers, in all your various guises, including the one as you sit here now: school blazer and fresh innocence...

He is still looking, to see how I am taking it. Dare I open up the field a little, and give him some encouragement? 'Aren't you going to tell me about it, then?'

At first he looks as if he might demur. There is a pink flush in his face, he is bothered, and ineffably sweet. Now he takes courage and leaps in, his hands fiddling self-consciously with the things on the table in front of him. 'I was on a beach, and there you were in the distance, by the water's edge. It's crazy, isn't it, to be dreaming about the sea in Meriden, which is supposed to be the centre of England? Anyhow, there we were, on this beach, and no-one else about. I waved and shouted your name – your first name – but you didn't hear me, and when I looked again, you'd gone, and all I could see was the tide coming in up the sand. That's all, really.' In his embarrassment he doubtless believes I'll find it girlish and sentimental.

But there is a strange icy sensation up the back of my spine: this boy must be psychic. 'How very odd, Piers.' It was my beach you saw, and I was there, exactly as you described it.

'Why? D'you think it means anything?'

It would be fatuous to reply that all dreams have meaning, but how can I tell him that *his* indicates his frustration at being without me, just like mine, at being without him? But we are too far into it, now. I privately made a rule to be candid with him, and now it is my turn to feel perplexed, like one required to give an account of his religious beliefs in public. 'I expect you wouldn't believe it if I said that the same thing happened to me.'

His mouth drops open. 'Really? You dreamt about me, Mr Millan?' The eagerness is as unforced as it is delightful.

I look him in the face, fearing to discover some possible treachery there, some slyness all ready to denounce me, but I see no more than an amazed naiveté which gives me the spur I need. 'First, I'd rather you called me by my first name. After my undercover research into yours, earlier on, it's the very least I can offer you in exchange.'

'I hoped you would say that, Roland.' The boy's polite formality is so sweet, but now there is a new look in his eye – satisfaction – as if having deftly completed a manoeuvre of his own making.

In a low voice, as though passing on some piece of vital intelligence, I briefly relate my dream about him coming over to me in the Minster, omitting mention of the kiss, and he does not take his eyes off me for a second.

'You missed me too, then? That must be the meaning, mustn't it?' Again, a boy's forthrightness carries us a stage further along our path. 'You see, I missed you awfully, Roland. Although we'd only met and talked properly once, when we had tea here, there were all those times at services, when - '

'When our eyes talked?' I pitch it as lightly as I can, but we both know the great volume that, as yet, has to be left unspoken.

'Well, why not? That's how we knew we were going to become friends.' He has obviously worked it all out in his long, boring time alone. 'I mean, I don't feel you're an uncle, nor are you like Father, so it must be a special friend, mustn't it? Even if we haven't known each other very long, I feel I'm fond of you already.' Scarlet-faced, he gallops away now. 'It *is* all right to say that, isn't it, Roland? If we both want to be friends...'

Suffused at this moment with such warmth that it must be visible, I struggle to find the words to answer this piece of artless sincerity from a boy who shows such remarkable perception and maturity of feeling. 'I'm fond of you too, Piers, but perhaps we should talk about it in a more private place. And I have nothing against our being special friends, though not everyone might agree.'

'Oh, do you mean - ?' There is a new and rather knowing look in his eyes, and I am terrified that our whole relationship might founder here and now on the rocks of the forbidden. Is he about to initiate the sort of talk about men and boys that the dirty-minded revel in? But the look has gone already: he realises that he tried to cut a corner and lead us into dangerous channels. Maturity topped with impetuosity!

'What I mean, Piers, is that your schoolmasters and priests might not permit you to make such a friendship with a total stranger.'

'But, Roland, you aren't a total stranger, not now, because you've told me things about yourself, and I've told you about me. And I like coming out to tea with you because I can get away from school and everything.'

'You don't hate it that much, do you?' Said with tongue in cheek, but fire in the heart, for he shows a talent for rationalising even the improbable, and saying just what I want to hear!

'It's awful, they keep us under, they hardly let us out, except now, and then we're supposed to stay in twos. We aren't even allowed to look round the Minster, because they march us everywhere.'

I accept the cue with gratitude in my heart, and a smile on my face. 'Might this mean, Piers, that you'd like us to have other meetings?'

He is wonderfully earnest now. 'Of course I would – I *do!* If not, we'll miss each other again, won't we?'

If necessary, I shall move heaven and earth not to lose touch with this incredible young man. 'Look, I've an idea. How easy is it for you to get out at night, after lights out?'

His face is a picture. 'I can get out of my room all right. We seniors have our own ones... And once we're all tucked up in bed, there's only Paget on call during the night.'

'Paget?'

'A drippy student, who gets all the jobs no-one else wants. He gets extra pennies for baby-sitting us! But the front door's always locked at night.' He leans forward, for we are speaking almost in whispers now.

'What about the windows?' I marvel at my audacity, as though some kind of baroque elopement were under discussion.

'All barred.' He is rueful. 'They don't trust us at all, you see.'

'Doesn't the back of your school connect with the cloisters, and that little alley which runs into Priestgate?'

'Yes, but there's another door that's kept locked.'

'Could you... get hold of the key to it, just for a short while?' I almost choke on the words.

We had overrun our time, and he was going to be late, but we fixed the final details regarding the key before he paid the bill and hurried away, with a shy backward smile at me. Somewhen, during an innocent cup of tea together, we had sealed a bond.

It had become obvious that Piers and I shared a need both highly unconventional and, as yet, beyond words, reaching out for something still in the dark and perhaps quite unattainable, a blank impassive wall like the west front of the Minster, where this had all begun. I could not see forward, and it comforted me that I did not even want to. And *he?* How far ahead could he see? In my happiness, I knew only that I wanted the present time to go on for ever, I didn't want my boy to grow up, grow away, take up his place in the outside world. All that we could do now was allow things to work themselves out, just as in the book I was reading. Except that... *Death in Venice* did not end happily.

*

A good hour after the sun had set, leaving a conspiratorial band of orange in the sky, I parked the Mercedes on the north side of the Minster, close by the railings that marked the edge of the land belonging to the Choir School. The dark shape of its building showed between the trees, and there was a light on downstairs. I felt very tense about the business with the key. *He* might pass it off as a bit of Boys' Own adventure, but I had got him to connive, and thereby put him at personal risk. He had duly dropped the key in the cloisters, as the boys trooped through for Evensong and I, hidden in the shadow on the far side, retrieved it when nobody else was about, taking it to the hardware shop nearby, where sharp tools obligingly carved into brass, while boys' voices sang psalms in the Choir... Within minutes, I had placed the two Yale keys in another spot in the cloister, where they would be safe till Piers returned.

He had only to let himself out now, and steal through the dark to where I sat waiting for him. The clock struck half-past ten, my heart pounding with the deep, echoing bell-notes. My mind was still bewildered by the speed of events, hardly able to believe that, after only two meetings and a brief correspondence, we had admitted a mutual fondness and planned this secret rendezvous. So far, he had been so unquestioning, as though our mute converse of looks had already prepared the foundations, and a force, not of our making, was pushing us together.

The estate agent had shown some surprise when I appeared minutes before closing time, to discuss making an offer for "Stella Maris". The owner was not so easily reached...

'But when I took the lease, you were only too willing to push the cottage at me for a sale.' Thank God, the Swiss and the French didn't do business in such a half-hearted fashion! I told him to wire my bid through, making it plain that I would pester him until I got an answer.

A tap at the window made me start. In the dim light I could just discern the whiteness of a face. I unlocked the passenger door, and Piers climbed in beside me, accompanied by a fresh smell of toothpaste and soap, which I found faintly disturbing. He had even put some gel on his hair which, with his jeans and black roll-neck sweater, made him look much older, as if he was dating a girl.

'Hullo. You made it all right, then?' Did he notice my gauche-ness? I started the engine and drove away, aware that I had not yet used his name.

'Yup. Nobody spotted me. Hey, what a super car, Roland. I forgot it'd be left-hand drive. Do you know, I always look out for it when we're practising up in the Song School before services? It was hell one Sunday when I was expecting you, and you didn't come. You probably won't remember that, though.'

I remembered all too well but, for the present at least, was not ready to match him in his nervous eagerness and excitement.

'Where are we going?' He had dropped the chatty tone.

'Just a short drive. Mustn't keep you out too late.' Now that we were seated side by side in a car, the traditional place of seduction, I saw only the obstacles already beginning to spring up around us. This just could not be! We were playing with fire...

'I wouldn't mind if we stayed out all night!'

It sounded like a joke, but I knew at once that he meant it. We had stopped at a traffic light, his face was turned towards me, the light from a shop window reflected in his eyes, and the deep stirring inside me turned to fear, for he was completely in my power now. *Or was I really in his?*

At last we are alone together, Piers, where no man can hear or interfere, and I yearn to utter my feelings for you. The light shines on your hair, I want to put out my hand to touch it, to make a physical contact more deliberate than the casual brushing of our hands in the tea-shop the other afternoon.

'Piers - ' He is waiting for an answer from me. He did say 'all night', didn't he? I thought I had trained myself to play by the rules, and now my intended avowal sticks in my throat. 'We've only met a couple of times. Some people might think...'

The lights had long since turned to green and a car was hooting behind us. I let in the clutch and pulled away, leaving the other standing. Piers looked back, but he did not smile. 'Roland, I don't care what people might think. When I first saw you looking across at me... well, it didn't worry me at all, and it doesn't worry me now.'

*You* were the one who started it all off, with that first look, but I shan't fluster you by mentioning that.

Piers had the bit truly between his teeth now. 'You see, I knew you were wanting to make contact with me, and that it wouldn't take long... Sorry if I'm sounding big-headed, but I feel I've always known you, ever since the start, and that makes it all right, doesn't it? And I do trust you.'

Unable to believe my ears, I am seized by a new and delicious sense of daring. 'Why did you think I wanted to contact you, then?' *What should I want with you?*

He looks down, not at me any more, patting his thighs lightly with his palms. 'I know it's not the way other people go on. It's different, with us. I guess you could call it a sort of attraction – oh, don't get me wrong – but I knew there was going to be something like that. I wasn't sure what, at first...'

He sounds like one lost in a maze. 'And are you sure now?' I cannot resist asking him that.

The narrow streets left behind, we are racing along a broad straight road out of the town. Ahead, the line of street-lamps abruptly ceases, and beyond, in the darkness, a great tract of countryside lies waiting for us.

'Yes,' he says quietly. 'And it's serious, isn't it? Have I got it right, Roland?'

The car speeds on, as though carried by something intangible, the spark that unites us. The cornfields gleam in the after-glow of day which, out here, seems brighter than in the town. In my mirror, I see the great black bulk of the Minster receding, loosening its influence over Piers and me. He has finally articulated it, has realised that we are already way beyond any notion of mere fondness for one another: he, whom I have only just got to know as a late twelve-year-old in cap and blazer, a young choirboy with a clear treble voice, is suddenly displaying a remarkable maturity. He nearly used the word "love" just now, though such love as I am feeling cannot mean the same to him, a child on the threshold of adolescence, but still by no means through the door. What would he know, as I do, about the entanglements which can dog a male-male relationship? He's obviously a decent kid, well brought up... Now my mind is getting entrapped in a morass of half-questions.

He is looking at me, anxious to see what my reaction will be, and I wrestle with my conscience. Why not come straight out with it, and to hell with constraints and rules? Surely he could cope with it, welcome it, even? Is this at last the cue for me to put into words my painful and deep feelings for him which, till now, I have not dared to hope he might recognise or answer? The ever-recurring question is whether he would be shocked or amused, if I did.

All my questions lack answers, and, not for the first time, cowardice wins. 'There are many different kinds of relationship,' – how lame that sounds! – 'ranging from quiet friendship to the most fiery passion. It's a scale that has no barriers in Nature, Piers, but men divide it into watertight compartments: affection for one's parents or one's marriage partner, and so on.' Even in my clumsiness, I have so far managed to avoid the word 'love' like the plague. It must sound to him like a priest addressing a couple about to get married, and I think I detect a smile playing on his lips.

Turning off down a lane, I bring us to the river bank, a peaceful and unfrequented spot which I once stumbled upon when taking distant camera shots of the Minster. In front of us, the last of the light in the sky glimmers in the slowly moving water. As if tacitly admitting that we are on thin ice, he opens the door, gets out and finds a tussock near the water's edge. 'We can sit down here, Roland.' It *is* serious, then.

Slowly, I move over and join him. As we sit next to each other, there is no sound to be heard, beyond the hammering of my own heart. Can he hear that, too? In desperation I take the plunge, as though into the river. 'Look, Piers, of course I find you attractive. In fact, I'm not ashamed to admit to some very special feelings for you.'

I can tell he is neither amused nor shocked by this. In fact, he is pleased. 'Do you know what "Platonic love" means?' I go on hastily, fearful of the way this situation is gathering speed. "Platonic feeling" would mean nothing to him. We are on the thinnest of ice now!

'Yes.' His low voice bears the tiniest trace of disappointment. 'We did it once in a Latin lesson. It's a distant sort of thing, as if - '

'As if what?'

'Well, as if you'd stayed on your side of the Choir and I on mine. But we didn't, did we? I mean, here we are sitting together and not distant at all.'

Well reasoned! 'That's right, but, you see, I don't really know you closely enough yet, to gauge what your feelings are.' Or how they may be developing. Now, in this piece of theatre we're engaged in creating, I've handed you a cue, but you can have no inkling at all of how things are with me, and what it all might lead to. I feel like adding a cautionary 'In any case…' but my lips refuse to form it. He does not need to be reminded that we are a man and a boy, in a dangerously close situation.

'Roland, you don't have to fish about. I always prayed that you'd come down out of your stall in the Choir, so we could get to know each other, and be together, just like this.'

Bright lad, he has accepted my prompting, and we are embarked on a game, the outcome of which neither of us can possibly know. He takes an audible breath now, and edges nearer to me, a decision evidently just made. The movement is discreet, as if he hopes I won't notice, but it gives the atmosphere of conspiracy a keener edge. And now he puts his arm round me in an affectionate hug. 'Is this wrong, Roland?' He is looking me right in the face.

My eyes burn and I begin to shake. He must notice that! 'Of course not, Piers, if that's what you - .' If that's what you really want. After all, it isn't me leading you on, but the other way round…

This time he puts both his arms round me, his breath is hot on my face. 'I meant it when I said I trust you, Roland. I'm not frightened. I mean, Christ, we - .'

We *what*? Do you mean *We're a couple of men*, and such people sometimes do certain things? The invitation in his tone is unmistakeable, his body is warm against mine, his young form full of vibrancy and life, and I am in danger of becoming a lost soul… Giddy with the heat of the moment, I wrestle with an inner wisdom which tells me to rebuff him, put an end to the madness while I still can, but he is so fervent now, so earnest, as if to say, 'We've got to make the most of this; we haven't got long.' The fragility of this budding relationship both charms and saddens me, for my own knowledge of all these things is so much wider…

His forehead is just below my face, and, because it seems the most natural thing in the world, I plant a kiss on it, exactly as I did in my dream. Only to reassure us both… But Piers raises his head and, without warning, kisses me full and hard on the mouth, leaving us both gasping. 'I've been wanting so much to do that, Roland. You don't mind?'

The buzzing in my head is worse, the tranquil river bank and the boy beside me fade out, to be replaced by vague, dark forms – demons with horns and grotesque faces. He has just offered himself to me in the most unmistakeable fashion. In my anguish, my chest begins to heave and I come to myself, sobbing like a child in his arms, my tears wet on his face, but he does not recoil. 'It's all right, Roland.' There is a mixture of comfort and surprise in his voice. 'Really, there's no need to cry. I love you, you see.' He takes the silk handkerchief from my top pocket and dabs my face with it.

Between my sobs, I blurt out how empty and futile my life was when we parted after Easter, and how utterly lost and miserable I would be without him. As I do so, a great burden lifts from me, as though all my sins have at last been pardoned. In this blessed state, we remain sitting there, each with an arm round the other.

'Roland, does it always affect people like that?'

We no longer need to speak in code. He understands, that is the miracle of it. 'Only when it's really deep, really powerful.'

'Have you ever been… like this before? Oh, but you must have.'

'Never like this, I promise you.' And that is God's truth.

It is as if we are two lovers, come to this quiet spot for a moment of intimacy, but how can I determine how far he is capable of sharing this experience, without cheapening it, demeaning him, relegating him to mere boy? And yet he is not like any of the other males I have known – how, at his tender age, could he be? I am so frightened by this, so scared by the desires which his kiss has ignited in me, that I have a duty to tell him how risky this is, how we will both be out of our depth very soon. *How I yearn to sink with you!*

Something splashes in the reeds on the other side, and I begin to withdraw my arm, but Piers clings on and smiles up at me. 'I'm not going to let you go, Roland. I want to be with you all the time. Can't you take me away? Mother and Father wouldn't mind, if I told them I was with such a good person as you. And I know you must be good, because - .'

His face is pale in the purple twilight, the eyes big, the hair falling over them. 'Because?' I can only whisper it.

'If you were hard or cruel, or something, you wouldn't have got upset like that, just now.'

He shares my impulsiveness, he is tempted by the impossible notion that I might somehow pluck him out of his indifferent school and the dusty world of the Minster... and I am in the grip of an indulgent idea: that if he and I were now to fly away like angels, nothing particularly strange would have occurred. How many men, if offered such a rare chance as this, would not seize it? What was life, if it did not allow a person to grasp at true happiness, now and then? He has responded, he has shown his feelings for me, and the barriers are down at last, a path cleared ahead. In this situation, anything and everything might happen in the name of love. My existence lifts out of its trivial plane, the world and its troubles melt away, and I see only Piers, want only Piers. Despite the almost insurmountable difficulties, we are embarked on a love affair – that much we both realise.

I look at him. There is emotion in his face, too, as he waits for me to speak. 'You're not a child any more, Piers.' That much you have shown me.

'No, and I think I know what I'm doing. I meant the things I said.'

But this only reminds me again of society's strict taboo on such matters, and my heavy responsibility for him. I need time to think things over, to repeat in my heart all that has passed between us this evening. 'We mustn't jump the gun. A really loving relationship has to be allowed to grow, and it's the better for that. I don't want to return you to your school, but we have to be practical.'

'You won't go and drop me now, Roland? I haven't scared you off?'

'What do you think?' We go back to the car, where I help him in, as though he were a woman one was fond of. Closing his door, I can see his face through the glass, pale and yet with fire in the eyes. The boy I take back is a very different one from the boy I brought here.

During the drive, I am tempted to remind him that we still have an enormous amount of things to say to each other, but he must have worked that out for himself, for he suddenly says, 'Roland, where do we go from here? With us, I mean.'

Already there are dots of light on the road ahead. You've been reading my thoughts! 'We shall make more plans, I'll see you every day at a service, and we'll continue to meet in the tea-shop, of course.' I was about to add the cottage to the list of assignation places, but caution stopped me. 'I don't think it's safe for you to sneak away in the evening like this too often.'

This provokes the first piece of defiance from him. 'Let them catch me if they can!'

'No, because that would put an end to our meetings altogether... And you mustn't smile at me so openly at services, or people will begin to notice. Discretion is all!'

Already we have reached the edge of the town and I can see his face, sporadically, in the light of the street-lamps. He looks mournful now. 'It's not easy, hiding your feelings, I mean.'

He doesn't yet know that a man has much stronger feelings than a boy, so I have more to hide...

The dark form of the Minster church looms above us, as I bring the car to a halt exactly where I picked him up, hours ago it seems. 'When then, Roland?' His hand is on my arm: he wants me to take the initiative.

'Can you get out tomorrow afternoon?'

'Tea-shop at five?'

'All right. Now you'd better be going.' I lean over and kiss him on the cheek. 'God bless you, Piers.'

He presses my arm and returns the kiss. 'Look, Roland, my window is the one up there, on the corner. I'll flash my light on and off to let you know I've got back safely.'

He jumps out, closes the door and is gone. I sit there stunned, unable to believe that what passed between us this evening was not just a dream: Piers, my love, my lover even, (for the kiss which he planted on my mouth as we sat by the river was surely something pent up, like the ardent release of all his longing and waiting in lonely nights – a state which I knew about all too well.)

I saw the fresco on the ceiling of the Sistine Chapel, where the finger of God touches the finger of Man, and a charge leaps across: the moment of Creation. In our brief private meeting, a seal had been irrevocably broken, as though virginity had been lost – but I could not tell whether mine, his or both. It seemed absurd that I, after my experiences of the world and the flesh, could still have anything left to lose, and yet I had: Piers had awakened something pure and holy in me from the very start, perhaps a portion of my own innocence that had never really died, but only lain dormant till now. Maybe I saw myself in him, years before, with all the fresh and eager promise of youth, the bloom still upon the fruit. Perhaps I had fallen in love with a mirror image.

And yet it was not myself that I saw, for I loved him as a separate being with his own emotions and affections, a boy who had not only responded to my admiration and love, but had even thrust beyond what I would ever have deemed possible: Piers the choirboy, Piers the gymnast, Piers the schoolboy, had stepped down from his pedestal, for me. And this gave way again to unease, when I thought where our hugging and kissing of a few moments ago might have led us. We were talking of Plato one minute, and the very next he was quite fearlessly engaged in what looked very like the makings of a physical love affair.

Sweat was on my brow, as new thoughts and visions crowded in. It disturbed me to think that this child – no, not child but youth – in jeans and sweater had come riding in my car, all ready, it seemed, to pursue a particular line. Did he not know that, in a dark secluded lane, lovers' hands inevitably turned to searching and caressing? He, the boy, and I, the man! Allowing his impetuosity to sweep me away, I had almost lost control of myself. It must not happen again...

Wrenching open the door, I leapt out. The evening air cooled my damp forehead like a blessing, and as I looked towards the dark outline of the school building, the light snapped on and off twice at his window.

He was safely back, then, but safe from what? And what would he be thinking, now? Would he gather friends round, to regale them with what had just happened, or would he see instinctively that it would destroy him, too, because the others were part of the world outside us, a society that would never understand?

But now I am assailed by new doubts: didn't it all run just too easily for comfort, for belief? *Did* I dream it? Am I dreaming still? Shouldn't there have been some kind of hesitancy, some reluctance between us, face to face like that, some kind of sparring, some hostility, even? No! For amid the potential shame and guilt of it, there's the irrepressible triumphant sense of having descended into the arena, a rare and golden chance, more than either of us would ever dare to dream of. Piers and Roland, and let the rest of the world fade away into insignificance and oblivion...

This boy is a sweet creature, genuinely affectionate with me. We are very, very deep, it seems, far deeper than friends or even family can be. And he deserves whatever I can give him in the way of love. One thing is clear, however: I must win the battle to remain in charge of myself, and of any situation where we are alone together, so that neither of us need ever have cause to hang his head.

*

The boy sat on his bed, doing a kind of action replay in his mind. I only know I want this man, - it was like that, the very first moment I set eyes on him - and I want him to keep with me now, whatever happens. He isn't like any other man I've ever come across. He cried, and I had to comfort him like a child, almost as if he's my equal and not a grown-up at all. He must know I understand about certain things, - he said I'm not a child any more - but would he understand about this sensation I have, which was never there before this Spring... partly an itch down in my body, partly a sort of daredevil feeling in my mind? I don't want to scare him off - he's obviously proper - but I have to work these feelings out, not on my own but with someone special. Not a girl, yet, nor any of the other boys here. There's something about Roland - a fine sort of feeling. He got upset when I kissed him, but he didn't reject me because of that. I know he missed me, over Easter, because he said so. I know he loves me, and I don't think he minds if I lead the way a bit.

I want him so much, I'll do whatever he wants. I told him that. It may be wrong of me, but I'm desperate for this adventure. It's the first time in my whole life that I've been able to do something really important, by myself.

And if it's with a man? I don't care: Roland is so special, it doesn't make any difference – *he is him!*

*

In my dream that night, a plump little cherub was chanting 'I love you! Let them catch me!' but then it transmuted into my former wife, repeating, 'You know what that means, don't you? How can you let it happen? I am going to save you from yourself.' A man looked out of the window at a gondola skimming past, and vomited into the canal.

When I awoke, drenched in perspiration, I knew she was right, as she always had been: I couldn't let it go any further, couldn't cross any more forbidden lines.

But then... I was half-way through buying the cottage, "Stella Maris", for him – no, for us. And wasn't it true that Piers had taken the initiative right through, ever since the first time his eyes dwelt on me in the Minster? *He* notched up the passions last night, not I. I'm not a boy-hunter, then. My boy is hunting me.

## *III.*

I pour some tea and push the biscuits across, trying as always to conceal my inner excitement at the revelation I am just about to make to him. 'I rent a cottage out in the country. Didn't mention it before because I couldn't see any hope of us going out there together. But you did say you'd like to stay with me, and I thought... if you were free over the Whit holiday...' My deliberately casual tone is intended to mask the fact that I have been rehearsing this overture but, when it comes to it, I am almost breathless with anticipation. Easter was a washout for me. 'Or... are you off to another relative?'

'Roland, I'd love to, of course I would. I'm not going to anyone else, this time.'

In their uniforms, they look so young, so untested. Is this really the same boy who sat last night with me in the reeds? But he has just said he'll come to stay. 'For the whole week?' I can scarcely contain my impatience.

'Sure, if you'll have me!'

'Do you need to get anybody's permission?' There are still rules to be observed.

'Oh, I'll write to my people. They generally let me stay with friends. No-one else needs to know, do they?'

How well he already understands that!

'Oh, by the way, Roland, the Head called me in today and told me my marks have improved enough to apply to Keatwells next year. Can you guess the moment when I stopped fooling about at school and started to work properly, for a change?' He grins at me across the table.

'I hardly dare imagine.'

'It was when you came into my life and started taking an interest in me.'

I congratulate him, while privately hating the transitory aspect of life, which brings you something, only to take it away again. Of course I must accept that Piers' prep school career, along with his treble voice, is limited, that both will probably end together. Common Entrance, and a new path leading up the hill to manhood. I went through all that, myself...

As if reading my expression, he leans over and gives me a comforting tap on the hand. 'We've still plenty of time before term ends.'

There is an impishness about him today. After all, we both know now that he is no longer the pure and serene child I thought him to be, in the early stages. As our bond strengthens, new facets will appear in him for me, obliterating his public image, and I shall be able to take pride in the fact that this is mostly my doing.

'Will you take me to the cottage very soon? I'd love to see it.'

'We'll pop over tomorrow evening, if you can get away again.' Fool that I am, to be always galloping ahead!

'Can I sleep there?' His eyes are big.

'Not yet. It's... not quite ready.'

He fails to conceal his disappointment at this. I think he knows I'm hedging, but for the time being he must simply accept it... Already I can visualise him roaming around in the gardens, the paddock, the dunes, down on the shore. How would it be? Certainly not father and son: he has already got us summed up quite differently. Special friends, then. Perhaps, in the end, we would manage to blur over our received and inhibiting concepts of right and wrong, smooth out the great gaps in our ages and experience, and legitimise what promises to become an unconventional and potentially perilous association. The world would say 'No', but the world's opinion will not be sought!

*

We had crossed, in the twilight, the low line of hills that lay several miles to the east of the town and, as the car's headlights picked out fleeting images of trees, hedges and farmhouses, I noticed a scent upon the warm night air streaming in at my open window: the salty flavour, betokening that the sea was not far distant. I wondered if Piers, at my side, was aware of it also. Then, when a road sign with the name of a well-known resort was caught in our beam, he quickly looked round at me. So grown-up, again, in his roll-neck...

'Just where is this cottage, Roland. Not near the sea, by any chance?'

'Since you ask, it's right on the coast.'

'On the coast? Do you mean to say that dream I had - ?'

'Yes. Odd, isn't it?'

'And you never let on about it, when I told you?'

'It didn't seem the right moment,' I said quietly. 'Anyway, I planned to surprise you, and I think I possibly have!'

I thought he might be cross with me, but he chuckled. 'Roland, are there any other things I ought to know?'

Yes, but not yet. If we don't take things gently, we shall get into real hot water. My head had begun its silly tricks again.

Although it was late when we arrived, he spotted the paddock and insisted on going out to the point where the sand encroached through the fence. A cold wind from the sea blew our hair about as we stood side by side, just as we had done on the river bank. A sensation of dread threatened to engulf me but, as if he knew, he linked arms with me.

'Is it possible to hire a horse here, Roland?'

'I expect so. Can you ride?'

'It's one of the few good things my beastly school lets us do.'

'I'll get you one while you're here.' Already I saw my boy riding along the wet sands at dawn, leaning forward, mouth open, eyes bright with excitement.

'You laughed. What's funny?'

'Oh, just having an outrageously romantic vision of you cantering along the beach.' To my astonishment I had, within minutes, become warm, secure and inexpressibly happy.

'Do you often have romantic visions, then?'

'Sometimes. Occasionally, one even gets used in my work.'

'You never really said what it is you do.'

We went back indoors and put some lights on. I told him about my designing for the stage, and produced some of my drawings for the restoration of the mansion. Piers took a polite interest for a while, but it was the cottage itself which really enthralled him. 'Clever, the way it's been altered about.' He nearly wore out the glass patio door, which slid into the wall at the touch of a button.

'The owner did all that before he went abroad. I may make some changes myself, if -.' I had nearly let the cat out of the bag!

In the kitchen, he reacted as if he had never seen a modern cooker or sink in his life. 'School's still back in the dark ages, and my old aunt's place is even worse!' In the lounge, my record cabinet caught his eye. 'Got any organ music?'

'Do you play the organ, then, as well as sing?'

He shrugged. 'Mr Baines lets those of us, who aren't too bad on the piano, have a go. Don't you have any Bach on record? All these seem to be opera.' But then he turned his head, and the look on his face expressed a new wish.' You haven't shown me upstairs, yet.' He got up, took my arm, and my sensation of dread returned.

'It's not all that interesting, really, Piers. The two bedrooms and their bathrooms are pretty much identical. I think the English term is *en suite.*'

But he would not be fobbed off so easily. As we paused on the landing, he asked 'Which one will be mine?'

'Here. This one.' Talk about marking out one's claim!

He tried the lamp over the divan bed, pushed open the bathroom door and looked in. 'I've even got my own shower and toilet,' he said, coming back. 'You've no idea how different all this is from the prison I live in. It's so homely here. School stinks.'

'I do know what your sort of school's like, Piers.' I went through all that, aeons ago.

'Hey, where did you go? You weren't a chorister yourself?'

'No. It was a toughish place in Yorkshire. Plenty of rugger, not much music.'

'You didn't like it, then? Did you go on to university?'

'Ended up at art school.'

'I'd like to go to university one day.' He looked out of the window. 'Can you see the village from here, in the daytime, I mean?'

'Just the top of the church tower in the trees, especially if the sun picks out the weather vane.' I steered him back to the landing. 'And opposite the bedrooms - .'

'*I want to see your room!*'

I opened my door, put the lights on and let him go in first. He did so slowly, almost cautiously, as if entering a sacred spot, made straight for the bed, sat down on it and bounced a little. The marriage bed. Barry, Fiona. 'It's a big bed,' he said, looking round.

'Just an ordinary double.' I knew I was buying time, not wanting to get on to the subject of my past life yet.

'I like your room. May I peep into your bathroom?'

'It's exactly the same as the other one!'

But, like a small child who loves to compare two identical copies of the same book, page by page, he had to look. When he came back, he was grinning. 'Not quite the same. Your bath's got a spider in it!'

He discovered the old door on the landing, opened it, and looked into the attic that I used as a lumber room. I flicked the switch and two wan unshaded bulbs illuminated the dusty beams, the piles of cases, trunks, odd pieces of furniture and pictures.

'Gosh, it's beautiful. If... the cottage was really yours, what would you do with it?'

'Renovate it and open it to the public. What do you think of that?'

'Really? Would I be able to help?' He had taken me literally. I put a hand on his shoulder. Avuncular again, far removed from shame or guilt. Perhaps it would be better like this. 'When you come, you can have a go in the garden, if you like. As the tenant, I'm supposed to keep it tidy. Or don't you like gardening?'

'I'll do anything at all,' he said, and there was a look in his eye that bothered me, though I did not know why...

I looked at my watch. 'Better make a quick drink, then we must be off. What would you like? Cocoa? Chocolate?'

But Piers was grasping my elbow. 'Please, Roland, please, don't let's go back tonight. I want to stay here in "Stella Maris". You do want me to come at Whitsun, don't you?' He had obviously noticed my hesitation. Was he using that as a threat? There was a slight tremor in his voice.

'Of course I do. You know that.' I hugged him closely to me.

'You see, you told me the cottage wasn't ready for me yet. But it is. The beds are made up. Everything we need is here. And you know I trust you, Roland. I'd do *anything* for you, really. *Anything.*'

There it was again – *anything* – and it hit me between the eyes. 'Piers, can you understand if I say that *we* aren't ready, just yet? We've... exchanged our words of affection, but it doesn't do to be hasty, in these things. I don't want you to feel that you're being railroaded into anything. Do you see what I mean? A relationship, especially like this one, takes time.'

I knew he would think I was talking rubbish and, for one moment, he looked ready to crumple, but then he took a deep breath and said, 'Yes, I see, Roland,' in an unspoilt way which, amidst my relief, I found admirable.

We went down, and I made cocoa.

'I very much want to see the cottage and gardens in daylight, too,' he said, but not reproachfully.

'You shall. They won't run off, you know!'

'Roland...' His expression was mirrored in his voice, and my heart turned to stone, so much did his every mood affect me. 'Does anyone else come here? I mean, sleep here? With you? I know I shouldn't ask...'

He was jealous of me, and I was both charmed and amused. 'I swear that nobody else comes here, and nobody else sleeps with me.'

His mouth dropped open. 'Hasn't anyone at all, ever?'

'There were one or two in my distant past, but I'll tell you about them some other time.'

'Is that why you have a double bed?'

'Yes.'

'And...' The child was grappling with a new thought, but finding no elegant way to express it. 'Were you in love – with those women, I mean?'

I could have laughed aloud. Women. There was only one of those... And then the thought froze in my mind. My love is not the sort you will know about, Piers, or are you half-way there already, and testing me out?

'You will always tell me the truth, won't you, Roland?' He had at last reached a theme that was very important to him: the staking-out of one's territory.

'I promise that I shall always tell you the truth about myself.' There, I've thrown in the towel already, and accepted the risk that I shall one day come out with something that will frighten him off. 'Now drink up. We must be on our way.' The lighting in the lounge was subdued, the chairs soft. I was as reluctant to leave as he was. He put down his mug, came over and knelt in front of me, took my hands in his and kissed them.

'You are a very good man, Roland, and I thank God that we met.' He rests his chin on my knee, and looks up at me.

I ruffle his hair very gently, and find I am blinking. He raises his head, I bend forward and our lips meet. Steady now. Where is the manly decency? Too easy to let oneself go, fall over the edge, sink with him to the bottom of the gully, relinquishing all scruples and fears. Soul and soul, Piers and Roland. *Anything* is an alarming concept whose implications must surely still be alien to him? The kiss seems to last an eternity, I feel worlds spinning past me, as though we are in a totally new dimension. Life stops, everything stops except my heart, which pounds on until my head aches.

I open my eyes and see his, very close, looking at me. There is a flush in his cheeks. I draw away, bothered by what we have just done, but he smiles at me, his full, open smile with those moist lips that have just been pressed to mine. 'It's all right,' says the smile, 'you needn't feel ashamed at all. It's quite natural, because we love one another.'

Getting up, I take the mugs through to the kitchen, my inside in turmoil. He follows and helps me to wash up, but this prosaic activity does nothing to appease a sudden great need on my part, here, in the sacred confines of my own territory, to make a statement to him: 'Piers, I have to tell you this, because it means so much to me. You'll see why... I'm reading a story by a German writer at the moment, and it's all about two people a bit like us – a man and a boy, who meet in Venice.'

'How can anybody else be like us?' There is a rare truculence in his voice.

'It's like this: one day the man is in St Mark's at Mass, and the boy is kneeling at the front of the church and, among all the chanting and the incense, he turns his head to look at the man, because he knows he's there, watching. Well now, there's that moment in the Eucharist when you go up to the altar with the rest of the choir, and I have to stay behind. It's really hard for me to be so far from you, in the Minster. The only thing is that, when I take the chalice, I know that you have just held it, and... do you understand?'

He stares at me, for my emotion has got through to him. 'I never thought of it like that, Roland. Like sharing, only special... Next Sunday, just after I take the wine, I'll remember what you said, I promise.'

We went out to the car, I turned on the engine and lights. He was very quiet as we drove back, and I knew that it was chiefly sadness at having to leave the cottage. Not that he was the type to sulk. I think the strong feelings that gripped me when we were physically so close must have affected him as well, and exhausted him, for he nodded off until we reached the Minster.

Piers was marvellous, asleep. A street-lamp shone in on his pale face when I drew up. His hair was over his closed eyes, and he looked so young and innocent that I was reluctant to touch him, even if only to wake him.

As the car came to rest, he stirred and opened his eyes. I put an arm round his shoulders. For a moment, his look was wide and wild, but when he realised where he was, and who was holding him, he smiled at me sleepily. I kissed him on the brow and he kissed me back on the cheek.

'I'll be at Evensong tomorrow, Piers. God bless.'

'You too. Oh, and – what was the name of the man in your story?'

'Gustav von Aschenbach. He was a writer.'

'And the boy he loved?'

'Tadzio.'

'Thanks for taking me to your cottage, Roland.' He was about to proffer me a hand to shake, but then thought better of it, and instead climbed out. We were back to the formal here, in the shadow of the Minster, where the niceties of etiquette had to be observed.

'Don't worry. We'll go again! Till tomorrow, then.' Piers waved, and vanished into the darkness. I sat there for a few more minutes, as usual going over things in my mind and trying to make sense of them. Then, when his light flashed its reassuring signal, I drove reluctantly away. We had, in a sense, crossed a watershed tonight. My boy was not an angel, he even seemed anxious to break some of the rules. I knew now what was in my own heart, but was only dimly beginning to guess at what might be in his.

*

Full of a burning sense of daring, he sat naked on his bed, cross-legged, staring down at himself. We kissed again, on the lips, and that started you off, John Thomas down there, just as the thought of it is doing, now. All those people who come to the Minster think we boys are so pure! They don't know the half of it. We're human, just like anyone else, under our robes. Christ, I'm fed up with the shamminess of it. When I leave this place, I'll gather up all the holiness they've tried to put into me, and drop it down a deep pit.

He rubbed himself in hot delight, wondering if Roland ever did that, too. What would he say, if he knew? That it's not dirty, if you are thinking about the person you love? A plan began to form in his mind...

\*

*My darling Piers,*

*It was nice to get your letter and hear your news. Daddy and I have talked about your wanting to stay with Mr Millan over Whitsun. Because he is a friend of your Headmaster and has invited two of you, we are ready to say yes. Daddy says you are old enough in any case not to get into scrapes.*

*If you are going to stay for the whole week, we think you should give your host a nice present (you will doubtless know what he would like), and I am enclosing a cheque to cover this..."*

\*

The three weeks to Whitsun dragged by, although we saw each other constantly: Piers in the Minster, his lovely head rising above the chorister's ruff, his clear voice singing the occasional solo; Piers, twice a week in the tea-shop, a schoolboy in a blazer, talking with me across the table about all manner of things – the nicknames and idiosyncrasies of his teachers, the tantrums of the organist-choirmaster at their daily music practice, and various amusing aspects of life in the School. It was all coded stuff, of course, ostensibly avoiding any deeper message, but his eyes, often intense in the discreet gloom of the café, suggested a myriad unspoken hopes and aspirations, all of which concerned us.

\*

It was during our visit to "Stella Maris" in the second week that I finally capitulated. We had been listening to music side-by-side on the settee in the lounge. It was warm and cosy and we were relaxed, affectionate and happy.

Suddenly he said, 'Roland, we're going to stay here tonight. Don't say no, because it won't make any difference. I've made up my mind for both of us!'

I looked down at him. 'And what happens when they find out at school that you've done a bunk?' I was not a little disturbed by this new tone, and the possible implications behind it.

'They won't know. We aren't woken till seven. You could get me back before then. Please, Roland. You do want to, really, don't you?'

What tenacity! But I could not deny that nothing was more important to me now than his delightful company. 'All right. I'll put a hot water bottle in your bed to air it, and I'll dig you out some night things.'

With a look of glee, he pulled a toothbrush out of his pocket.

'You knew you would be staying, you cheeky monkey!'

He laughed out loud. 'I brought it along, the last time we came here.'

Perhaps it should have eased my mind somewhat that *he* had chosen to take the initiative, but I was privately alarmed at the way things seemed to be heading. We went upstairs, and I let him choose pyjamas.

'Not too bad for length, are they?' he said, holding the trousers against him. 'I won't need the jacket.'

'You'd better get ready for bed now, if we're to be up early. I'll set the alarm for half five.' I took refuge in the practical, adopting a parental tone which was not my own.

He groaned. 'Never mind, it's worth it. You *will* come and say goodnight, Roland, when I'm ready? I think I'll have a shower, if that's all right with you.'

'I'll bring you a hot drink, when you're done.' As I went downstairs to the kitchen, my apprehension was already infused with a new excitement. To have Piers sleeping under my roof was something I had looked forward to, as one anticipates the end of a depression and the beginning of a golden age; but, now that he was here, the reality of it bore down on me, and I was terrified, as well as intrigued.

I took him a mug of cocoa and a hot water bottle. He was standing by the bed, wearing just the pyjama trousers, his bare chest and arms pink from the towelling he had been giving them, his hair still tousled. I handed him a comb.

His youthful form fascinated me, despite myself. His well-shaped chest and back slowly regained the pallor of his face, his nipples were pink and small, his navel, just above the trouser band, a dark and secretive little recess.

His arms were long and quite slender and, as he raised one to comb his hair, I saw that the armpit was still smooth and bare. His whole body emanated a radiance and freshness which, at such close quarters, was almost overwhelming. After placing the bottle between the sheets, I sat down on the edge of the bed, and he flopped down beside me. *That was my second mistake this evening.*

Nakedness is a barrier between people who are clothed and those who are not. He does not seem to sense my inhibition, and puts his bare arm round me, while drinking his cocoa. I can smell the fresh dampness of his hair, I can scarcely resist the temptation of touching it with my lips, full of the sensation that a warmth is rising from his body, enveloping me in a vapour, arousing my desire.

Piers sees my alarm. 'Roland, what's wrong?' Is that innocent concern in his voice? Ashamed of my feelings, but afraid of upsetting him, I bend down to kiss his upturned face on the forehead. Where is the harm in that?

But the slit in the front of his trousers has sagged open, his soft parts are visible, and I suddenly cannot cope with it. For once, I envy Aschenbach, who stopped at his beloved's door but went no further. Before I can leap up, though, he has put his arms round my neck. I had only meant just to kiss him goodnight, but his lips seek and find mine and, as he holds me tightly to him, my heart is racing. Then as his breath comes quick and hot against my cheek, there is another, new sensation: his lips part, and the warm moist tip of his tongue is searching the outside of my mouth, demanding entry! A satyr has me in its grip and I am lost, doomed to the sweetest perdition a man can know.

I am in a swoon, my lips relax, and his tongue, like a hard little snake, finds its way inside, and I taste the sweetness of the cocoa and the fresh, hot savour of his mouth. On the point of taking him in my embrace, I suddenly come to my senses. This is dangerous, it goes beyond all reason. I, a free spirit, am being trapped, seduced even, by this boy! I draw back, gasping for breath, and his grip eases. Piers, Piers, where did you learn *that?*

His face is scarlet now, and there is a hard glint in his eye that I have not seen before. Piers, the faun. Piers lusting. He lies back with a half smile, looking me up and down in triumph, his trousers still gaping open, but in invitation now. For the soft part is soft no longer, but a pink pillar topped with its red rosebud. *Where is the innocence, now?*

I kneel down by the bed, tug at the waistband to cover up the temptation, and rest my forehead on the bedclothes. 'Piers, if our love is to become physical as well, I'd rather we went more slowly.'

'But isn't that what you want, too?'

I raise my head and look him straight in the eye, and he takes my hands in his. 'I know some things about sex, but I don't know everything yet. Will you tell me? I'd rather it came from you.'

I know that, even in this state he is being entirely honest and serious, and it falls to me to be the same. 'Give me time, and I'll tell you what you want to know – about marriage, too. But it's love we should really be talking about, Piers. Sex is only a part of that. You mustn't try to run before you can walk. Besides…' We are a man and a boy. How could it possibly work?

'Are you married, then?' It is his turn to look shocked now.

'I was, briefly. Now, slide under the covers and get some sleep.'

He looks disappointed, but does as he is told. Then another thought occurs to him: 'Did you have any children?'

'No.' There is relief in his face that he has no competition for my affection! 'Pray for us, Piers.' I kiss him lightly on the cheek, and then turn to go.

'Roland…' His tone stops me in my tracks. 'Am I awful?'

'How could you be?'

'May I ask you one very last personal question? *Did you get a hard, too, just then?'*

I take a huge breath.

'You did say you'd always be honest with me.'

'Yes I did.'

'You mean you did say, or you did get one?'

'I'm not made of stone, Piers.'

'Nor am I! It's all right, then, if it happens for both of us!' Triumph in his voice.

I knew he dearly wanted to discuss it further, but I cut it short with a 'goodnight', fled to my own room and, trembling with so many conflicting emotions, dropped down on my bed. I did not know where I was, knew only that I adored Piers from the very root of my being; but what had just happened between us seemed to buffet that love, instead of strengthening it. Was it just prurient curiosity on his part, to find out *what one did?* I was bathed in sweat, and there was a disturbing stickiness against my thigh. I got up, undressed wearily and went into the shower, running it cold, to chill myself to the marrow. Then I dried myself with a rough, comforting towel and sat down on the bed again, whispering his name over and over again, all too aware that only a thin wall separated me from him.

This was strong, heady wine, and I was unused to it. Was he, or had his innocence already been plucked away at that school? I had to protect him, protect both of us, and steer the whole business into calmer waters. Perhaps the very idea of his coming here at Whitsun would need to be knocked on the head.

I climbed into bed, but although my body was relaxed and I soon fell asleep, my mind was not at peace. In my dream, he and I were in a dark, narrow alley between the crumbling red-roofed houses that clustered round the Minster.

Looking up, I saw a purple night sky, a solitary gas-lamp hissing at the corner. We crouched in the shadows, furtive and fearful of discovery, hands and lips searching each other's body. Above our heads, a bell boomed out its message of warning, but his relentless fingers pursued their purpose, seeking out the secret, tender spot that yields the fruit. My limbs arched like trees bending in a great wind, and I awoke, sweating and groaning, polluted with my own essence.

I was ashamed as never before. Wet dreams had never bothered me in the past, but this one had been so real, so true, so near the mark, as if the boy and I really had pleasured one another in the very shadow of the spiritual powerhouse that brought us together in the first place. But what sweet violation!

Then, recalling that Piers was sleeping in the next room, I sprang out of bed and locked my door, full of remorse that this was not right, and could not be. When had I last wept into my pillow? Never, in my most intimate moments with Barry and Jonathan had I suffered such qualms as now. With them, I had been an equal, we shared the responsibility for all that was between us. Here, with a boy whose loveliness deeply disturbed me, I was more vulnerable, more easily tempted, and more likely to succumb than ever before. Had he not given me the plainest possible invitation?

Of course I desired him in a physical way as well, - I would be deceiving myself if I did not, - but I had forgotten exactly what a budding adolescent is capable of. Was it possible that Piers, divested of his chorister's robes and blazer, was a young and beautiful demon, (like those who tempted the angels as they passed through the twin cities of vice), sent to deprave me in the one taboo field which I had never yet entered? And could all this really have sprung from a harmless exchange of glances, so many months ago, it seemed, across the Choir? I had to admit that the road ahead, despite glimpses of light, remained obscure. I could not, did not want to, see too far, lest we should find ourselves trapped in an *impasse*. I was too weak to withstand many more assaults on my emotions, and sooner or later the last bastions of restraint were bound to fall.

We drove back through a countryside that was grey in the dawn. He yawned a lot and seemed hardly to have awoken from his sleep. I was tense, conscious of him beside me, yet unable to chat normally, as if all was well with us.

'You're not angry?' he said at last, as we crested a rise and caught sight of the distant towers on the skyline.

'I love you, you know that, Piers. Love simply cancels out everything else. It can't be so easily killed.'

'I only did... what I did, because I love you too.' His voice faltered. 'I would never think of it with anyone else.'

'Weren't you just a bit curious to see what might happen?' I said, aware of the touch of irony.

He hung his head. 'That's why I asked you if I was awful.'

I managed a smile. 'People think when they get to my age that they're immune from being shocked. It's a bit of a revelation to find that the outer skin is still soft.'

'Christ, I didn't mean to shock you.'

'It's all right, Piers. Just a situation I haven't ever found myself in, before.' Despite last night's performance, I think he is still as inexperienced in life as I am!

'Is it very bad, us being together and loving each other like this?'

I stopped the car, so that I could look at him properly. 'The world, if it knew, would condemn it, as it always condemns things it doesn't understand, or things it secretly covets. I don't see that it's wrong for any two people to love each other. Love doesn't work to order, it doesn't always stick to the conventions. For me, love is as important as life, and much, much more important than other men's traditions and morals. But I expect you've been brought up to reject all that I've just said. I'd understand, if that were the case.'

'I don't like running with the rest of the herd,' said Piers quietly. 'Otherwise I wouldn't be here now, would I? It's funny... You read in the papers about boys being abducted, but they never tell you any details about what happens to them. I mean, if it was always like this – like we are – what would be the problem?'

I struggle to control my voice. 'Piers, those men are vicious. They want only the physical side, the baser aspect of it, and they harm their victims immeasurably. They don't love them.'

'Then why do boys go with them, if they're so awful?'

This line of questioning was tormenting me, but I owed him the best answer I could find. 'Because they are wooed with all sorts of promises, and they don't realise what they've committed themselves to, till it's too late. I assure you, Piers, that my feelings for you are quite different. I see you as a whole person, a soul as well as a body, and I *love* you as a whole person.'

I was afraid that, in my attempts to stay on the side of the angels, I was getting him out of his depth, but he nodded, took my hand and gave it a squeeze. 'I'm just so happy with you, Roland. You're what the French call *sympathique*. Do you know French?'

'I hardly speak anything else, when I'm at my home abroad. *Je te remercie, Piers. Tu es bien gentil.*' And he understood what I said.

We arrived just before sunrise. He slipped away into the passage that led to the cloister and, a few minutes later, waved at me out of his window. I parked on a terrace overlooking the lower part of the town. The misty blueness in which the houses lay was turning to pink. The circle of the sun came up slowly behind the wooded hills on the other side of the valley, shining its golden light into my eyes. The Minster clock chimed the three quarters, and I was reminded of a very different scene, of passion in the darkness, of the hissing gas lamp and our groans of delight. In the warm light of sunrise, the ghosts melted away and, with them, my inner turbulence. There was no need for me to fight against my nature any longer. Piers understood how things were, and he was not afraid. I need not have worried whether he could cope with our relationship. We wanted and needed each other, and we were bound by a force outside ourselves.

I looked round and saw a statue glinting in the sunlight, newly set up on the gable of the Choir. Would the One, who gave so much, take this splendour away from us? I was captain of a ship unmoored, borne out to sea on the breeze, into the unknown, happy in the knowledge that Piers was its sole passenger, and oblivious to all possible hazards and storms. Never before in my life had I been so conscious of being here on earth to tread a path, to fulfil a mission that would lead me to truth in the end.

\*

He was surprised by my refusal to return to the cottage in the days before Whitsun. The excuse was the pretty watertight fact that some work had to be done on the car. He had to be content for us to meet a couple of times in the tea-shop instead. I had explained why I never invited him to my rooms in town, for they represented only a very makeshift sort of home.

I spied on him constantly. He was aware of me at services, of course, but he did not always notice me at other times when, for instance, I would hover, after Evensong, around the shops near the Minster. One afternoon, just before we were due to meet for tea, I was astonished to glimpse him coming out of a jeweller's, and had to bite my tongue off not to ask any probing questions about that, for it was hard to accept that my boy might do things that were no concern of mine.

'It did occur to me,' I said, as we sat at our usual table, 'that it would be wiser if you took a taxi to the station after your service on Sunday, and then I could pick you up there.'

'Glad you suggested that, Roland. I had visions of having to hang around outside school with the other kids all gawping at us. That wouldn't have been a very good start! By the way, my parents dropped me a line to say it's OK. Don't forget, we're being let off immediately after the Eucharist, as we've been such good boys and sung so sweet, like!'

\*

Whitsunday, at last, dawned bright. When they processed in at the beginning of the service, there was a special light in Piers' eye that said 'Today is our special one!' I blushed to the ears, as if the thought had been spoken aloud, here in the sacred heart of the Minster, in the presence of choir and clergy.

Until Piers came on the scene, I had known little or nothing about adolescent boys. One saw them doing paper rounds, playing football, going to the cinema with their girl-friends. He fitted into no category that I knew of, which only served to enhance my feeling of empathy with him and, what was more, he managed to embody all the qualities I most prized: he was responsive, attractive, remarkably mature emotionally, and possessing a rare beauty of the soul – tender and thoughtful, and yet not cissy, nor pitiful nor weak. He had an inner strength that showed in his every gesture as he stood there and sang. I worshipped him as something divine, not a creature of mere flesh and blood. Happy the man who was loved in return by such a being!

Today, the Choir is a blaze of flowers and white and gold vestments. The candle flames tremble as if in excitement. I am at the wedding of Piers and Roland. The priest gives him the Cup. He sips and then, getting up, turns and deliberately catches my eye. With beating heart, I approach the Sanctuary, as one who is to be joined to another as surely as in the marriage rite. The chalice which touches my lips links me to him. I return it to the priest and look round at my love. He nods back, and the ceremony is complete. *Those whom God hath joined, let no man put asunder.* Piers, Piers, the days of empty longing and lonely nights are nearly over. Ahead of us blazes a light which will envelop the two souls now united with one another.

But a doubt blots out my joy: honeymoons were attended by fear of the unknown. Piers would cope with anything – he had said as much. But I? The adult in the relationship should be the strong one, the leader, but there were too many ghosts in my cupboard still. The lapping of water outside the window had once given me an excuse to go out on the balcony and look at the canal below. Darkness, fetid odours from alleys and dirty water. Lights in windows opposite, where cramped apartments filled crumbling buildings.

'Roland.' With a summons in her voice, she was waiting for me to perform a duty, lying on the vast, uncomfortable bed. A marriage without humour, without love. I had in fact told her very little about myself, but she seemed to have guessed a thing or two. I knew very well that Fiona hoped to redeem me, like a painting to be restored, a patient to be cured. Success might have killed her interest in me, while failure would be an admission of defeat on both our parts. I vomited into the canal. You cannot unmake a man, just like that. There is blood that flows, flesh that lusts, a mind that is occupied by images that will not yield. Fiona tried, but she did not lift even a corner of the painting. I had married her just to salve my conscience for my dead mother's sake, but I knew that it would be doomed from the start.

Now, as I pause at the altar rail, I am in trepidation again. It is not the thought of physical contact with Piers that frightens me, but rather the unspoken convention that a union has to be satisfied on the wedding night. The world, and one's conscience, expect it, even if both partners would prefer to come to it by easier paths in their own good time. Hell, can't we banish such spectres from the cottage?

Must we be bound by rigid ritual? Are tenderness and love to be thrust aside by the pagan, instinctive need to get the pound of flesh straight away? Before witnesses... Blood on the sheets... Honour satisfied.

My earlier elation has vanished, as if invisible barriers have grown up, to prevent us from viewing each other in the same way, or being at ease with one another any longer. His talk of men abducting boys shocked me, and yet, by roundabout ways, I am the abductor after all, waiting for a pure and innocent lad to finish singing here, before whisking him away secretly to spend a week at the cottage with me, a man twenty-two years his senior and whose only reason for getting to know him is a deep-seated passion. Is my intention with him not abandoned and utterly selfish?

At the moment when I begin to drag myself back down the Choir, the organist begins a loud and triumphal march, instead of the more contemplative music that usually accompanies the Communion. In my despondency, I keep my gaze averted, even though piercing, jubilant trumpet notes are ringing all about me. I should be holding my head high and looking at him proudly, for the game is over now, our looks and words need no longer be cloaked in euphemisms, hesitations, politenesses: we have constructed a language in which everything means only "I love you", and it would make no difference if the rest of the world were to collapse around us.

I fling myself into my stall and kneel, wondering what I might try to pray for. Reassurance? Strength? Or gentleness? And what is Piers praying for, over there? We must be psychic, he and I, for, as I finally make myself look up, he raises his head, smiles across at me, and I have the odd sensation that a tongue, like a snake, is searching for a way into me, bringing with it a magic spell: everything is going to be all right between us, and I need fear nothing more.

## *IV.*

Piers wasted no time in shaking off the choirboy image. As soon as we reached the cottage, he rushed upstairs with his case and, in a few seconds, the scholar in blazer and flannels was transformed into a young god in pale blue swimming trunks, leaping over the paddock fence and racing me through the dunes. The sea was sparkling and oily smooth on this day of joy and sunshine, and we swam a long way out together, until the broad sandy beach became a narrow yellow strip.

He began a wrestling game, in which we grappled, splashing and sinking beneath the waves amid peals of laughter. His lips, when they managed to connect with mine, were wet and salty, his body smooth and cold in the water. With his hair clinging to his head, he looked like a seal.

We swam back, and while I towelled myself, he ran off, dripping wet, his beautiful form moving with grace and ease, to look for flotsam along the beach. Tadzio had come to life before my eyes…

'I love you!' I shouted into the breeze, and he heard me, waved, came running back, and we lay down together on our towels.

'This is fantastic, Roland.' Grains of sand, like flour, were sticking to his wet body.

'You look like a sea monster,' I teased him.

'What about you, then? Have you seen yourself? You've got seaweed in your hair!'

'No, I haven't!' I felt about with one hand.

He dropped a feathery dark piece of it on me. 'You have now!' I had never seen him playful like this, before.

Although it was a summer's day, the breeze was making him shiver. I wrapped a towel round him and hugged him to me. He smelt of salt and wind and freedom. I kissed his hair, his ear, his neck, found the little dimple at the throat and planted another there. In return, he passed a hand over my chest with the delicacy of a woman caressing her lover, pushed the tip of his finger into my navel and waited, to see my reaction. I gently ambushed his hand and kissed it. 'Steady, now,' I whispered, though there was no living thing for miles, save some gulls shrieking through the air.

As we walked back through the dunes to the cottage, arm in arm, I was consumed, not for the first time, with an urge to tell him something important, in this case what my glance back at him from the Communion rail this morning had meant to me. 'It was as if we had just celebrated our -.'

'Our what?'

I had blushed crimson, but I was sure he knew what I meant.

He spluttered with laughter, I let go of him in panic, but he grabbed me again. 'Look, I'm not laughing because what you were about to say was daft... Oh well, it's a secret for the moment, but you'll see!'

What a genius he had for putting me at my ease! 'You know, Roland, if you'd told me in the middle of a street in town that we'd just got married, it wouldn't somehow seem to fit, but, because it's here, it's just right. And I feel the same way that you do. Does it mean we can.. ?'

He was looking at me intently. We were approaching another watershed which, once crossed, would change us both for ever.

'Sorry, Roland, no. We agreed not to... just yet. Forget that.' He was covered in confusion as well as sand, and I found him inexpresssibly sweet.

We had a snack lunch, which he consumed like a ravening beast, then I drove with him to the small resort up the coast, to replenish the larder. He took charge of the supermarket trolley, and I let him choose all the things he most enjoyed. He went for pasta dishes, prawns and fruity yoghurt. When I added some cans of beer and bottles of wine, he laughed out loud, wanting to know if an orgy was being planned. I studied his face, but he meant it only as a joke – and I caught myself feeling disappointed.

We barbecued steaks in a corner of the garden that evening. Flames and sparks shot out of the charcoal, lighting up our faces as the darkness gathered around us. I asked him if he ever did these things with his parents, but he pulled a face.

'They aren't *fun* people, if you see what I mean. They'd never let their hair down like this. Mother was thirty-eight when I was born, and Father's four years older, and they've got their own lives, really. When I try to talk to him, he always seems to be buried in some book on archaeology. I think he's privately after a knighthood. Mother likes to go and visit boring people, and there are stacks and stacks of *them* down there. She doesn't really understand me... I don't like running my people down, but...'

But they obviously have very little time for you. 'Is that why they placed you in a boarding school?'

'It started when I was at the local primary, up in Scotland, and a teacher noticed I had a good voice. He told my parents, and they took the cue, and in no time I was doing cathedral voice trials.'

'Where did you live in Scotland?' I had always been intrigued by that slight trace of accent in his voice.

'I was born in Fort William, but we lived in Oban. Anyhow, they didn't think I stood a chance with St Paul's, or anything really prestigious. Mother of course wanted me to go to Winchester and Father favoured York, but in the end it was Wharnley – for better or worse.'

'It must have its plus moments?'

He turned, to look me full in the face. 'The most plus moment was meeting you, Roland. If I hadn't been at Wharners, it just wouldn't have happened. Do you believe in Providence?'

'Oh yes, but I don't call it that!'

'What then?'

'Fate, pure and simple.' My chief guiding force.

'Oh, I see. Don't you really believe in God, then?'

'I was brought up to, but I don't think I've managed to be much of a God-person in my life. How about you, with all your spiritual doings in church?' I had my tongue firmly in my cheek.

He did not seem at all troubled by what I said. 'I've started to go off it, in a big way. So that's something else we have in common: we're pagans!'

At this moment, a seed was sown in my mind, which I knew would grow in the days ahead of us: Piers, for all his polite deference to me, was always finding little ways to push us together. It was subtle, like the drop of water on the stone: 'Would it be a good idea if...? Do you think we might...?' It had of course begun that night when he had insisted on staying in the cottage, and I had found no valid reason to refuse him. I now suspected that he thought he had me in his hand. It amused me, it flattered me, and I did not see the need to put up defences because, at this early stage, it had not taken on the form of an attack. How it might develop was still a puzzle to be solved, certainly for me, and probably for him also.

Later, when the glow had died away in the barbecue hearth, and it was time to retire to bed (for we were both exhausted), a strange shyness suddenly took hold of us. He allowed me to tuck him up in his bed and kiss him goodnight (chastely on the forehead), and I felt like a father. He obviously sensed this, for instead of trapping me in his arms, he gave me a quick peck in return and settled down without question. As I reached his door, he said my name in his soft voice. I turned, and looked back at him.

'I love you. Thank you for letting me come back.'

My sleep that night was deep and untroubled. When I woke, it was almost seven, and the sunlight was coming through the curtains. Was it possible that he would be here under the same roof for a whole week? I had never had a boy to stay with me before, not counting that night which he so cleverly engineered. I could hardly believe that yesterday's service, the car journey, the swim, the shopping and the barbecue had been real. Closing my eyes, I sank back into sleep again.

The next thing I know is that my bed rocks, and a lithe, warm body comes sliding in next to mine. Bare young arms hug me, and moist lips kiss me. 'Piers!'

'May I stay?' His voice is very near, his breath on my face smells freshly of toothpaste. I look at him, see the anxious, earnest expression in his eyes: not a game, but a serious manoeuvre, for which he is awaiting my approval – and my terror melts away. 'I would have come last night, but I felt a bit shy.' Come for what – the honeymoon?

Never has anyone been more welcome in my bed than Piers Moriston. What follows now is done out of love, and neither furtive nor shameful. We embark upon a duet of lips and hands, caressing one another with tender movements, mouths murmuring words of love and kissing, our tongues playing hide and seek. And when this music reaches the point where we explore further, lying naked together, the passion and desire are mutual and unforced.

We are each surprised and intrigued by the other's body. He has evidently not seen a man naked before, let alone in erection, and his questing hands hesitate at first, until I show him. I, for my part, had quite forgotten that an adolescent boy, with only the faintest trace of downy hair between his legs, and with soft parts that are still fair and virginal like those of cupids in works of art, can nonetheless match the performance of a grown man in all but the final emission.

His body, as my tongue explores it, still tastes salty from our swim. He reaches his climax quickly, with the effortlessness of youth, and begs me to take him on to another at once. When I gently suggest that he should not wear out the mechanism, I am underestimating the potential of his age.

When his moment happens, there is nothing degrading about it, no hint, in his eyes, of the shame that I had always known in myself, but only a radiance more glorious than I had ever seen. I put my head on his chest, my cheek against his panting, clammy flesh, and hear his heart pounding inside.

'It's beating very fast, Piers.' A lover might have responded with some cliché, such as 'It's beating for you', but a boy of this age is too artless, too inexperienced in the subtleties. I think he is merely enjoying the discovery of lust, in an understandably self-centred way.

But that last suspicion is unfounded: when it's made clear that I have no intention of trying to mount him, he is concerned that I should not miss out. For are we not *married?* After some experimenting, I manage to come to my own moment clamped between his thighs. He never takes his eyes from me so that, when my groans fill the room, I am shocked to have made him witness the truly animal side of lovemaking, and to have allowed my libation to bespatter his body. But he assures me he doesn't mind at all: he is simply glad that it worked for me, too. He seems to be open to any new experience. Anything…

I pass him a towel and lie down next to him again. As the turmoil of my own lust and longing subsides, I see clearly, for the first time since I got to know Piers, what I have just done. This brings the tears, but he puts his arm round me, and strokes my hair with a comforting hand. 'Roland, what's wrong?'

'I led you on, Piers. That's what was wrong.'

He sits up, his boyish torso poised over me, and looks down into my face, like one in command of the situation. 'No, it wasn't wrong at all. And if anyone did the leading, it was me. I wanted this from the very first. When I saw how things were shaping for us, I prayed and prayed that we'd end up in bed together.'

'You mean you planned it all?'

'Don't look so stunned, Roland. I admit that I didn't know I *loved* you, from the first moments, but I was very intrigued by you. Simply had no idea what real love was like, you see.'

'But you have, now?'

'Thanks to you, yes.'

That was the plainest answer yet, to the question that had burned in me for a long time: how much of my passion for him was reciprocated? I had not, after all, taken an innocent, I already knew that the angel in surplice and cloak was very much flesh and blood, and not entirely ignorant of the secrets of adult men. He had sought me out, found me, taken the initiative even, and this did much to allay my guilt. In this first real act of love together, he had brought me a joy and release such as I had never known with any other person. Nonetheless, I now found myself prey to an almost physical aching inside, which I could not talk to him about, and which would not go away.

\*

The sea had receded a long way, the sun was just about to set, and he came cantering across the wet sands, the horse's hooves splashing in the rosy puddles of sea water. The camera whirred, recording moments of godlike beauty. His body, already tanned by the sun, exuded an elemental purity and mystery that surprised me. If I ever thought that I had explored the terrain that was this boy, I never knew it utterly: unknown aspects kept coming into view, others sank again into obscurity. The camera, at least, captured some facets of the essential Piers for ever.

He rode straight into the sea, churning up white water amidst the green. The horse threw up its head, threatening to rear, but he, skilful with rein and stirrup, calmed the beast, turned it about and galloped back to dry land. Boy and horse, dripping and triumphant, raced up to me, glorious in the light of the departing sun. 'We love you to bits,' he called, trotting off into the dunes, 'my horse and I!' and the classical picture exploded into laughter.

\*

He was looking at some of my designs, clothes in jazzy colours destined for fashionable male boutiques all round the world. 'They're just a bit of fun,' I said. 'By way of a sideline.'

When he discovered a drawing of a youth, olive-skinned, hair greased down, in a pair of exotically coloured Bermuda shorts, he said he liked it. 'Looks a bit like me.'

'He *is* you. I did a quick sketch at Evensong one day.'

'Gosh, I'd love to have a pair like that.'

'Come upstairs, then.' I went to my wardrobe. 'They were to have been a surprise for your birthday, but you may have them now.'

The Bermudas were white, and I had painted elaborate designs on them in oranges and mauves. Without embarrassment, he took off his clothes and put them on, looking at himself in the mirror.

'Marvellous!' He came over and gave me a kiss, just a natural gesture of thanks, which I accepted as such, delighted that we could be so spontaneous and close with each other, without necessarily going any deeper every time. He was not son, not nephew to me, not quite lover in the fullest sense, but a charming mixture, transcending all bounds and ties of blood.

\*

In a rare moment of indiscretion, I asked him the name of the fair-haired boy he marched in and out with, at services, and he turned on me. 'Why d'you want to know that? What is he to you?' We were sitting on the crest of the dunes, overlooking the sea. The sun was warm, the sand soft and inviting.

I was taken aback by the sharpness of his tone. 'Nothing, Piers. Merely that... when I found out your four names by reading them on your cloaks - .'

'Copes,' he corrected me, grimly.

'Yes, sorry... I had to juggle with – let me see, now – Whaley and Moriston and Cove and Fillingham, without knowing which one was you.'

'So you decided to interrogate poor little Squires,' he said. 'Bit sneaky, wasn't it?' The hard edge was giving way now to humour.

'I couldn't think how else to find out who you were. We hadn't quite met...'

'If you really must know about the blondie,' he said, with a trace of scorn, 'it's Filly, and he's a right little pervert. Don't you ever dare get interested in *him*. He's the big I Am, he's made it to big game already, even claims he does it during sermons.'

I displayed some feigned alarm at this revelation. 'Big game? You mean tiger-hunting?' He knew I was teasing.

'I mean sex! It's known among the boys as big game and little game,' he said airily, biting into an apple. 'Little game is – well – what I can do, but big game is when the spunk comes.'

It was my turn to correct him. 'Semen' was not yet in his vocabulary. He blushed. Unwittingly, he was stirring up in me memories of things long forgotten or suppressed. School, crushes between boys...

'A lot of that sort of thing goes on. There's a league table to see who gets from little game to big game. Filly organises it.'

There was a bitter taste in my mouth. 'As you said, it's just sex, just messing about. It's not love, it doesn't count for anything.'

'I know. I once tried it with another kid in the toilets, when I first started to get hard-ons,' Piers blurted out. 'I knew it was dirty, and afterwards I wished I hadn't... But it's not dirty with you,' he added hastily, to reassure us both.

I repressed a smile. 'Sex doesn't belong in the toilet. It deserves a better setting.' Even as I said it, I realised I had been coming out with things he might not have accepted from his 'beaks' - but he took them from me.

A seagull flew overhead, mewing to another. We walked to the water's edge and stood, with the waves lapping over our bare feet. He wore the Bermudas all the time now, and I was flattered. I asked him to run along the beach, and did some more ciné. He was a natural subject, quite unconcerned by the camera.

As we walked back up to the cottage, I could tell that he had something on his mind. 'Roland, how do you know when big game's going to come?' He was trying to find the right words, but I knew what he meant.

'With these things, no two people are alike. You just have to be patient, and it happens. Nature looks after all that.'

'How old were you?'

This time, I did not want to be open with him and reveal that puberty in that sense overtook me alarmingly early, during the London blitzes. I resorted to a white lie: 'Nearly fourteen.'

'Some people say it's wrong to toss off, in case you go blind or mad, or something.'

'That's just scaremongering.'

'We've got a teacher who's also one of the priests, and he gives little sermons to us about purity. In his last one, he said that "self-abuse" (that's what they call it!) is wasteful, and a dead-end activity. Filly said some very rude things about that, behind the scenes. It was the only time I'd ever agreed with him.'

He was stroking the horse, a grey supplied by a nearby farm. 'You don't mind talking about these things, Roland?'

'Of course not. It's right, to get them off your chest.'

'Do you… ever do it to yourself?'

In cowardly confusion, I shook my head, not expecting him to believe me. But, as if he accepted it, he swung on to the horse and rode bareback round the paddock. I was sure he must have noticed my embarrassment, but our talk had cleared the air for me. We had something else in common, then: before we met, neither of us had anyone to confide in, like this.

\*

It was a cruelly hot morning, without a breath of wind, the trees motionless in the orchard, the tar melting in the lane outside. Piers hurried out into the paddock with a bucket, to give the horse a drink. I made a lot of lemon squash, put it in the fridge to chill, then set up an awning and placed a couple of comfortable chairs on the terrace. From here, I could see him pottering about, talking to the horse, examining the fruit trees and, as the enthusiasm caught him, carting barrowloads of earth from the depression which I had been digging out; for I was allowing myself a little licence as tenant, and planning an ornamental pool, even though the negotiations for the purchase of "Stella Maris" seemed to be going nowhere.

His Bermuda shorts were in the wash, and he was wearing his jeans. His bare brown chest and back were sticky with sweat and streaked with grime, but there was a look in his eye which announced that he was idyllically happy. As always, my own eye was enchanted.

Mid-morning, he came to say that he would like to swim. There was a hesitancy there, which I remarked upon. With Piers, a cue was never to be ignored.

'Well, it seems silly to put on my trunks when my body's all grubby, and I don't want to mess up my shower, so would you object if I swam in nothing at all? There's never anyone around.'

I collected towels, then, discarding all our clothes on the terrace, we ran like two children to the beach. Piers did not stop, but hurtled down into the water, splashing it all over himself until he glistened in the sunlight. I followed, and we swam on our backs for a long time, our bodies like pieces of greenish-white plastic trembling and swaying with the motion of the waves. I felt free, newly born again.

'Piers, you once said you didn't like your name.' To me, it was the most beautiful one I knew, and always would be.

He turned his head with a grimace. 'They used to call me the ploughman at school.'

'Piers Plowman?' I liked that!

'Oh, it's all right when you say it, Roland.' He recognised the affection in my voice.

'You really do hate your school, don't you?'

'Most of the other kids get on my nerves. They're so narrow and childish. And the beaks... well, they're a pretty useless bunch.'

'Still, you won't have to put up with it much longer.'

He got some water in his mouth, and spat it out. 'I expect my next one will be much the same.'

'No it won't, because it'll be much bigger. You'll be sure to find someone congenial there.'

'Did you have *congenial* friends, at your school?' He was quietly ribbing me!

'More enemies than friends, I'd say.'

'Was it very dismal, then?' He had suddenly become serious.

'I was desperately lonely at times.' Mainly my own fault, of course, because that's the way I am.

'So was I, till you came along. Wouldn't you say that you and I are alike in lots of ways, Roland?'

'Well, yes... It can be difficult, without brothers or sisters, to have someone really close to talk to, about private things – don't you think?'

'Not if you've got a special friend, like we are! Roland, will I be able to see you now and again, when I'm at my next school? I'd die if I thought we'd have to finish it all when I leave Wharnley.'

'Of course we'll keep in touch, or I'd die, too, and then there'd be two corpses!' A large wave took us by surprise, and we emerged, choking.

When we regained the beach, the air was suddenly filled with a throbbing noise, and we looked up to see a huge helicopter bearing down on us. 'Crumbs,' said Piers, 'nowhere to hide!' He seized hold of me and, as the aircraft passed overhead, making our hair ripple, he rested his head against my shoulder. 'That'll show 'em, peeping Toms!'

\*

I adjusted a lamp, to soften the shadow of his chin. The lounge had become a studio, the big window closed against the cool night air, the curtains a backcloth to his incomparable head, framed in close-up in my viewfinder. There was a faraway look in his eyes, his mouth was open, the even white line of his top teeth showing. He was looking to one side, and downwards a little. I did not pose him formally, but, because he was so natural, took what I saw if I liked it, moving camera and lights occasionally, photographing him from different angles, with a variety of expressions: serious, smiling, laughing, mischievous.

'Aren't you going to take any full-length ones?'

It was an invitation to capture the god in his beauty, naked, with shadow playing the role of discretion and taste, while the strong hard light on head and torso brought out the statuesque quality. His body seemed to be totally elastic, and easily moulded to any posture I desired. I got him to stand with one foot in front of the other, and to curl one arm up over his head, while looking down at the floor. Then I made him turn his back to the camera, and stand with his left hand on his hip, the other hanging down. The light accentuated the valley down the back, the generous curve of the buttocks, with their deeper cleft between. If only I had a property sword and fancy hat and boots, I could have turned him into Donatello's bronze David! Finally, I got him to sit on the carpet facing me, with his legs drawn up, his chin resting on his knees, round which he wound his arms, and looking at me under his brows with a Puckish expression.

At the end of the session, he leapt up, pressed the button to open the sliding window and, naked still, danced out into the garden, along the terrace and into the paddock, where I heard him shouting and singing and slapping the horse in sheer exuberance.

His elation was sadly lost on me. I was beginning to gain an objective view of how things were working out between us during this week. He was not a child any more, though there were aspects of him which obviously had to mature, as was the nature of boyhood, but my own role had been something not really under my control at all. It was all very well leaving things to Fate to decide, but one ran the risk of forfeiting one's integrity. The net result was that a shadow had started to grow over our last days together, but I was determined that its gloom should not infect him also.

\*

The liquid in the tray trembled. We craned our heads to look at the sheet of printing paper as it slowly mutated in the dim orange light of my makeshift darkroom, strange black contours appearing among the white areas. Even as we watched, a face grew, filled the paper, - his face – with large eyes looking out at us. I took the sheet out of the developer and dropped it in the fixer. He was fascinated, not so much by his own attractiveness, as by the magic processes he was witnessing, where shapes evolved out of nothing.

'Can I see it, yet, with the light on?'

'Just a moment.' A minute or two later, I switched on the main light, ran the wash-basin tap over the print, and then handed it to him.

He smiled, rather self-consciously for once. 'It *is* good, Roland. I've never had a picture like that taken, before.' Narcissus was present in him, after all. Hadn't he gelled his hair, the very first time I took him out in the car? 'Can I keep it, please?'

'If you like, you can have copies of all of them, but how will you explain away the nude studies, if the wrong person sees them?'

He grinned. 'I can always invent a photographic uncle, or something. Will you do one of those, now?'

I selected another negative, put it, in its carrier, into the enlarger, focussed the ghostly image, switched off the bathroom light and enlarger lamp, and took another piece of half-plate paper from its box.

Within seconds, the new picture was forming in the developing tray, and I was surprised to find myself almost more excited by it, than by the boy who was its subject. Piers was beside me, warm, alive, full of boyish enthusiasm, but the naked form that materialised before us was classical, caught in a timeless plane, as though there was no link at all between the two of them. We had produced a work of art.

The young god stood, turned half away from the camera, but with his head facing towards the lens. The left hand was propped casually on the hip, the right one was at his side. He looked out from beneath his brows, his mouth open a little, and the expression was intense. It was both Piers, in the attitude in which I had seen him many times in the Minster, and a naked deity, whose head and shoulders were picked out by the light, the abdomen and legs remaining in silhouette, with some sidelight giving them just the suggestion of three-dimensionality. One saw that he was unclothed, and yet no-one could have taken exception to it: a picture to stifle criticism and stir the soul. As I switched the light on and held up the print, I could tell that Piers too was admiring it: I had opened his eyes to the wonder of his own body, to a boyhood beauty that went mostly unacknowledged in the world.

It was only then that the reality of what this meant to me rose up like a spectre: I had captured my Piers exactly as he was now, had frozen him in time, preserved his form against the disfiguring effects of development into adulthood. He was my boy, my cub, and I could not bear to face the prospect that he would ever evolve into something different from this. A little gulf had appeared between my Piers of the photographs and the youth at my elbow, who would all too soon go away and become a man, marry, have children and join the millions of tedious faceless folk that peopled the world. Where was there a place in all this for me?

*

He woke me gently. As I opened my eyes, I saw that he was no longer in the bed – our bed, now – but sitting on it, with the curtains drawn back. He put a finger to his lips, tugged at me with his other hand, and so brought me over to the window, which was wide open.

We stood there rather as we had done outside the gift-shop aeons ago, when I first spoke to him and risked breaking the spell. Yet it had not been broken, nor the mystery explained. Now he had woken me to show me the dawn, pink bars of light striping the dark sky, the trees still in silhouette. No sound, no movement.

We remained motionless also, as if looking at eternity. There was no need to say anything: it was all there, written in fire across the sky, and human tongue could not begin to give the measure of it. We stood before God, hand in hand, two naked children still innocent of the world, if not of each other. He had come to redeem me and, short though our time was, he *had* redeemed me. I lived in hope once more, my existence had taken on a new meaning. I cared, cared for him and myself, for life and its beauty, and strove to banish the foreboding in my soul.

At last, the fire grew in brilliance, and the edge of the sun rose in blinding glory. Piers turned to me, putting an arm round my waist in his affectionate way.

'I'm part of you now. Does it often happen that a man and a boy love each other, like this?'

'Not, not in the way that we do. It's more common for two men to have such a relationship.'

'Is that what's meant by queers?'

I shuddered inwardly. This was not a road which I wanted us to pursue, but he was not a person so easily fobbed off... We got back into bed, for it was chilly outside still, and cuddled up together. The intimacy gave me courage.

'Piers, I don't like labels. I hate being put in a pigeonhole, if you see what I mean.' Frederick Rolfe once said that labels were more lethal than libels – and he was right.

'But I'm the same as you, label or no label,' he said, without a trace of worry or disgust, clearly unwilling to leave the topic there.

'What I'm about to say will sound like a beak again,' I warned him.

'I don't care. Beak away!' But there was a seriousness behind the levity.

'Just because we've shared a bed together doesn't mean that you're necessarily like that. A boy your age, who's beginning to develop sexually, has to get himself orientated. He may form an affection for his own sex at first, but he usually grows out of it and discovers girls. If I'd thought for one moment that I was going to turn you homosexual in later life, I'd never have got so close to you, never.'

My formal tone ill befitted two people nestling together, and there was bewilderment in his face. 'What's natural and easy for us, Piers, might not be the same for another pair of males.'

'Are you *sure* you're like that? I mean, you aren't pansy or anything.'

His naïve but loyal tone amused me. 'It takes all sorts, and it's more obvious with the brassy or effeminate types.' The timid ones don't stand out.

'I don't think you're like that at all, but Hutters is. He's the assistant organist, and you can see it a mile off. And...' But he suddenly clammed. He'd decided not to bracket me with the queer set. I did not tell him that I knew better.

The sunlight was pouring in at the window, and there was a trembling red splash of it on the wall just above our heads, like a judgment, which disturbed me.

'You said you'd had... people in your life before we met.'

Hoping that a dash of truth might satisfy him and block any further inquiry, I took a deep breath, and weighed in. 'I once had a wife called Fiona – yes, she was Scottish – and then, at different times, a friend called Jonathan and then another called Barry.' It sounded so trivial on my lips, so absurd, so loveless.

'These men, were they your lovers?' He was obviously startled by the boldness of his own question, and I faltered, not knowing how to get us out of this predicament.

'Why d'you ask that, Piers?'

He had gone scarlet in the face. 'It's just that I think I have a right to know, don't you? What were they like, these people?'

I told him about Barry, who got himself into trouble 'over someone else, not me', causing us to part. This was definitely not the moment to be talking about prison. Without waiting to see his reaction to this, I then did a thumbnail sketch of Jonathan and his clumsy suicide attempt.

This time, he was visibly shocked. 'Do a lot of homosexuals' (how carefully and delicately he enunciated the word!) 'try and kill themselves?'

'Not so much, now that the law's been changed. It still gets on top of some.'

He suddenly grabbed hold of me in alarm. 'You wouldn't ever try that, would you?'

I kissed his bare shoulder. 'I think I have a pretty firm hold on life, and quite a big stake in it.'

But there were tears in his eyes. They welled up, trickled down his cheeks, and he pushed his face against my chest and sobbed. 'You'll forget all about me soon, and find someone else to love. You won't want just a *kid* like me, any more. I know it.'

'Listen, Piers, I shan't want anyone else, while I have you. There couldn't be anyone else to approach you. My love for you is unique.'

He raised his head. The beautiful eyes were red with weeping, and I felt triumphant that my beloved should be suffering on my account. 'You said that no-one else ever sleeps here, but those men you just told me about – did they sleep with you, *in this bed?'*

By 'sleep', we both knew exactly what he meant. I made a clumsy attempt to deflect this one, but he went remorselessly on. 'You live in Switzerland, or wherever, so who sleeps with you there? You must have someone. Is it a man, or a woman, or a boy, like me?'

He gave me no chance to answer this, but leapt up, ran out of my room and slammed the door. I followed after him, but he had already locked himself in his room, where I could hear him weeping uncontrollably.

I sat down and rested my head against his door, wondering if Aschenbach ever did that outside Tadzio's. 'Piers, listen.' But his sobs drowned out my soft cajoling, so I had to raise my voice. 'There is nobody else, I swear it.'

Amid gulps, he shouted, 'You love Filly, don't you? How can I trust you any more?'

Now I was beginning to get angry with him. 'That's just stupid, and you know it.' I was tempted to add 'You silly little fool.' This was a situation quite new to me, and I had no idea how best to handle it. All I knew was that the day, having begun so promisingly, was now about to collapse in ruins. I just kept talking quietly at his door – anything that came into my head, provided that it sounded soothing – and, at long last, he opened it and looked down at me.

'Sorry, Roland. I was being jealous, you see. I don't usually get like this.'

We went down together and prepared some breakfast. While we were doing it, I played a trump card. 'Look, Piers, I can demonstrate to you, if you like, that you are the only person I care for in my life.'

He looked at me curiously. 'How, then?'

'It's something quite serious, but you needn't get worried. You see, I've done quite well for myself as far as property and finances go. I don't mean to flaunt this at you, but you need to know. I have, for example, a stake in a couple of places in London, and a flat in Geneva. At the moment, I'm trying to buy this place.'

At the mention of the cottage, his face lit up. '*Buy* it? But that's great. Will you come and live here always?'

'That depends. Anyway, as you may guess, acquiring all this property is going to be an embarrassment later on, because… whom do I leave it to, when I die? I have no relatives left, no wife any more, no children, and, now, just one special love, - a young man called Piers Moriston, who wants to have proof of my sincerity.' I was being deliberately pompous, and continually watching his face.

For the first time since I had known him, he displayed a proud defiance. 'I don't want any of it, Roland.' The hardness in his voice made me recoil. 'I never loved you for what I could get out of you.'

This was not at all what I had expected. 'Then you wouldn't approve of the Will I have recently made, naming you as chief beneficiary?'

He shook his head, not just to say no, but in a way that indicated incomprehension. 'I don't want your things, Roland. I want just you.' He came round and knelt by my chair. 'You're mine, and I'm yours, anyway. I'd rather you left your things to the dogs' home, or whatever.'

He was right. I should have kept the musty odour of old documents out of our relationship. At least he understood my motives, and I was proud that he could be so unmercenary.

'Roland, I don't want to even think about death, but what is your life going to be like? I can't bear to think of you ending up lonely and miserable, and I know it gets worse in old age.'

At this, I felt a bubble of grief begin bouncing inside me but, for his sake, struggled to contain it. He was right, also, in his vision of the future, but wrong to think that he might do anything about it. After all, nearly a quarter of a century separated us. 'You are very sweet, Piers, to be concerned about me like this. But, as long as I have you, I shall be all right.'

He munched away at his cereal for a while, then said, 'Did you take photos of those others, the way you did of me?'

Oh God, it's as if he feels that I've raped him with my camera. 'No, I didn't.'

'Why not?'

'Because they weren't… so photogenic.'

This seemed to satisfy him. I had evidently managed to get the fact across to him, without using so many words. One cannot tell a boy straight out that he is beautiful, unless it is Oscar Wilde talking to Bosie! Then I had an idea. 'I do in fact have a photo of someone, up in the lumber room, that may interest you.'

Mystified, he followed me upstairs.

'It's rather like looking at the broken pieces of a beautiful vase,' I said, opening a cardboard box and taking out some photos, 'except that this one wasn't exactly beautiful.' Conscious of my awkwardness, I found the one of Fiona, and passed it to him.

'She was pretty. When was it taken?'

He speaks of her as if she were already dead. Pretty? Pretty forceful, endlessly probing into the soul. Not a secret left in me, nor a scrap of dignity. 'Sixty-three.'

'On a ship?'

'Suez Canal. Don't pick up your future intended on a cruise.' One tends to get carried away by a certain romance in the air, but it's all spurious, like a bad film, where the couple lean over the rail, looking into the sunset.

'Who's this man?' He was holding up a faded sepia photo of my father.

'I never really knew him. He went down with a ship in the war.'

'Do you think things would have been different for you, if you'd had him, all the way through?'

This piece of perceptivity took me aback. 'In my case, I don't know. Mother and I were always very close, there being no other children for me to compete with.'

Piers picked up another photograph. 'Is that her?'

It was the studio portrait taken six months before her death, as if she had known what was to come, but wanted to leave me with a message of hope and understanding. 'It's all right, dear,' her steady gaze said, 'I know you can't be otherwise.'

I turned my head away.

'She was pretty, too,' said Piers.

I got up and took him downstairs again, unable to stand another second of that kind of nostalgia.

We sat down together and, after a silence in which he seemed to be struggling to express what he wanted to say, he finally came out with it: 'Is intercourse between a man and a woman really as marvellous as it's supposed to be?'

Never, with Fiona. In the uncomfortable months of our non-marriage, I tried repeatedly, but flesh does not obey where the spirit hesitates. In the end, she became scornful, and killed the whole business stone dead. The inevitable annulment was swift – to the boundless relief of both of us

Now, my lover was asking me for advice that might set him up on the path I had abandoned. Were the keys to his future in that respect really in my hand? As his only confidant, whatever I said in answer was likely to have a marked effect on him. I was tempted to keep him, to hold him to me and model him on myself, harshly dismissing the other sex – but I loved him far too much to want to destroy him, like that. For a few minutes, I assumed the role of beak again...

\*

The sunlight had gone watery, clouds were blowing up, and I suggested that he might like, for a change, to come with me to Akington Hall. As we drove inland, I began to quiz him to find out how strong his faith might really be. He confirmed my early impression that he was tired of singing the ever recurring choral music, and that the endless round of services had deadened him to everything else. 'I used to think I had a sort of agreement with God – I know it sounds daft – but now I don't think he's interested in me any more. I made some promises when I got confirmed, but God doesn't seem to be keeping his side of the bargain!'

'Don't you believe that he brought us together, then?'

'I sometimes just don't know what to believe. How about you?'

He had deftly put the ball in my court. 'I had a Christian sort of upbringing, but some of the things that have happened in my life since then make me wonder if religion has really brought me any benefit.'

'But you go to church, otherwise you wouldn't have come to the Minster in the first place. Were you looking for what our priests call "spiritual help"?'

How acute! 'In fact, it was a hot day and I was just looking for somewhere cool. A verger collared me and put me in a stall for Evensong, and that was that.'

He chuckled. 'But you've come to almost every service ever since!'

'I think you know very well why that is.'

'Yes, and I wouldn't want to be there either, if you weren't.'

By the time we reached the Hall, a light rain had set in. I called at the site office, collected a couple of hard hats, and then we ambled around, with burnt débris underfoot and charred rafters gaping to the sky.

'Wouldn't it be easier just to demolish it and start again?' asked Piers, staring up at the men working high on the scaffolding.

'You'd be surprised. The walls mostly withstood the fire, so they'll be able to get a roof on before the winter.'

'But it's just a shell. What can you possibly do with that?'

I chided him gently for not having looked properly at my drawings. 'If you have enough money and vision, you can do anything at all.'

'Would you like to live in a place like this?'

'Wouldn't it be rather extravagant for one person?'

'You could have people to look after you, Roland.'

'I do have a part-time cook-housekeeper in my place abroad. But a huge staff of servants? No, I don't think that would be quite *moi.*'

'That's funny.'

'What is? Not wanting to live in a mansion?'

'No, the way you pop French words in. Will I be able to come and see you there, one day?'

'Of course.' My heart leapt at that!

'Why do you live over there, and not in England?'

I tried to explain to him how I felt that contemporary Britain was degenerating into triviality, that I saw it mainly as a place where money was made, but the arts were starved. 'People don't despise intellectual and artistic things in mainland Europe, the way they do here, and religion isn't being driven out either. Places like Wharnley Minster will just be dusty old museums before long. So it's better to enjoy the present, while we've still got it.'

He seemed to agree with that. 'Father says he hates all the crime here. Says that London's going just like New York. Have you been to the States, Roland?'

Just at that moment, Mr Whitwell, the foreman, came up to us. 'Morning, Mr Millan. Why now, don't I recognise this young man under the hard hat?'

Sensing trouble, I got him on to the topic of the temporary roof, and when it was going to be put on. Piers, red-faced, left us to it. When I had finished my chat, I joined him.

'D'you know who he is, Roland?'

'Of course I do, and he seems to know you!'

'He's the father of bloody Whittie, that's why. One of the sixth form boys at school. He boards. Not a chorister, though.' He took off the hard hat and looked at me. 'D'you think it matters that he saw us?'

'Why should it? You're on holiday, now.' But behind my assumed cheeriness was a small, nagging concern. I didn't want people to see us, either, and start doing mental arithmetic.

Whether he was really worried by this, or was still harbouring a grudge against me for this morning's upset, his mood had become sombre, his feet kicked through the ashes, raising a bitter odour, and I judged it wiser to make for home before our day was utterly ruined. Fortunately the drizzle had yielded place to the sun which had woken us with such ceremony this morning, giving promise of a good afternoon to be spent on the beach.

\*

'Why do men become like it? He did not mean it unkindly: he was merely curious. We had finished our meal and were in the lounge. The sliding window was open, for the sun had not yet set, and the air was still warm. I was relieved that he had regained his usual good spirits.

'I don't think anyone really knows whether people are born like it, or just acquire it.'

White and pink roses were shining invitingly among the greenery. We stepped out into the garden, descended the terraces and strolled as far as the paddock gate. The horse, always alert to our movements, came trotting over, and Piers stroked it, letting his fingers play over its soft mouth.

'The pansy types are born like it, aren't they?'

'Maybe it's some action of the glands during adolescence. It's a very critical time for a boy.'

'I've almost reached that time, haven't I?'

Since our first close moments together, he had blossomed and thrived, he seemed balanced and fulfilled, so that I imagined myself to be playing a positive part in his development. I, the educator! And, for his part, he had taken me through the whole gamut of boyish behaviour: affection, playfulness, seriousness, joy and grief. He was not a collector's piece, if anything he had collected me, had sought me out, to reward me with the great reserves of energy and love which he could not bestow on anyone else: his parents were too remote, his classmates too unloveable, his teachers too dull. I had risen like a star in his sky, and he had come to me, not so much to follow as to guide.

He was constantly surprised what a small part the physical side played in our life together. His appetite for it was enormous, and I had to restrain him, to prevent the currency from becoming debased: he, like a young hound seeking adventure, and I, full now of secret guilt, trying to get across to him the virtues of dignity, self-control and moderation! In this one week, our love crystallised into something which to me was simply beautiful, crossing the boundaries of age and experience, levelling away the discrepancies between man and boy, and fusing us into a new unit of humanity. On the one hand, I could see it as a moment of sublime happiness, that rare treasure that belongs only in paradise. On the other, as the sand in our hour-glass ran out, I was reminded that I was older and more experienced than he, that the path we had trodden together, though delightful to me, could lead him into the abyss. The memory of Barry was still raw.

'Piers, you must promise me something.'

Whenever the dark eyes looked at me, I melted. He had such a way of unmanning me, without even knowing it!

'Promise me that you will get married one day to a girl you love, and that you will never, never go with a man again.'

The breeze blew up a little whirlwind of sand on the far side of the paddock. He looked immeasurably hurt but then, seeing the anguish in my own face, took my hands in his, putting them to his lips, as though he understood exactly what I was going through.

'I swear that I shall never love anyone as much as you, Roland.'

I shook my head. 'That won't do.'

'All right, I shall get married, and you shall be the best man!'

I knew he was humouring me. He would never want me in *that* role... 'You haven't got a girl friend, yet?'

It was a silly question, and it made him explode with laughter. 'One at a time, wouldn't you say?'

The horse trotted away towards the dunes. The sun was nearly gone, and the wind was chill now. We strolled back past the pit which we had begun to dig, for the garden pool. Like various things we had begun here, it would never be finished now.

From the bottle of whisky in the cupboard I poured myself a good measure.

'Oh Lor, was that a bit of an ordeal for you?'

I admitted that the father role did not come naturally to me.

'You've taught me far more than a father ever could,' he said gallantly but, despite the compliment, there was a finality about it.

If I had helped *him*, he had uncovered parts of me whose existence I had never properly seen before. Piers and Roland in communion, each drawing strength and solace from the other, and making the grey world a touch more habitable. I had assumed, at the very start, that  placing another person on a pedestal and deliberately making him remote would very likely invest him with qualities not quite earthly, so that the moment of his descent from on high would be like the toppling of a statue, or the dissipation of a mystery into thin air: thus I had reasoned the early beginnings of my relationship with Piers.

The mystery, however, not only remained, but intensified from day to day. The nearer I came to him, the more conscious I was of not really knowing him at all. However frankly we spoke to each other, however closely we were entwined, emotionally and physically, I never possessed his soul, nor he mine. The fact that he was in many ways a closed book to me only increased my obsession with him, my vain and frantic desire to complete the puzzle, to know and encompass him totally. This boy, who lay in my arms at night, was almost as unattainable as if he had remained in his choir stall at a distance from me, and far more enigmatic and elusive than any woman could ever have been.

\*

I wandered through the cottage, calling his name, but he did not answer. There was no sign of him in his bathroom or bedroom, and the dust lay untouched in the lumber room. A kind of panic gripped me. I looked out into the garden and towards the paddock beyond. The horse was still there, alone.

I went out, still calling 'Piers', my voice weak against the buffets of wind coming in from the sea. The sky was streaked with dark clouds that swept in low across the land. Reaching the top of the dunes, I felt droplets of water on my face, like tears, but whether they came from sky or sea I did not know.

The dunes were lumpy, with hillocks and hollows, and tufts of sea-grass growing in the sand, which was white and powdery. The wind whipped up flurries of it, stinging my face. Mountains of spray surged and fell at the edge of a colourless sea, black water crested with angry white.

I walked about in the dunes, my heart as forlorn as the scene before me. He had deserted me, gone off without saying anything, and I was desolate, punished, not knowing where to turn.

Suddenly, coming over a ridge, I saw a hollow in front of me, a few yards away, at a point where the dune rose almost sheer. There, projecting out of the little cliff, was something grey: a bare foot, streaked with sand. He had been tunnelling, and the roof had collapsed on him.

I leapt into the hollow, and began scraping at the sand with my hands. I touched his leg and it was cold. I tugged at his foot, but could not pull him out. Like an animal, I tore at the sand, gradually uncovering his legs and thighs. He was lying on his stomach. Suddenly, the sand face collapsed again, and I had to burrow feverishly once more. I gasped, spat sand out, whimpered his name and, inch by inch, laid bare those cold damp limbs. Buttocks, back and shoulders.

At last, I seized his feet again, and gave a mighty heave. His body slid clear from its cave, I turned him over, wiped the sand from his face and put my head on his chest. No heartbeat. I put my mouth to his, to give him the kiss of life, but the lips were frozen, the nostrils clogged with sand, the dark eyes closed. He must have been dead for hours. His face was a terrible colour, the lips like a black gash in the features. His arms hung at weird angles, as if broken, and there was blood beneath his finger-nails.

I bent down, gathered up the chill body in my arms and, blinded by tears, stumbled back with it over the dunes. He was gone, lost to me and to the world, and it was all my fault.

I awoke, in a state of sore distress, to find Piers nestling against me. It was still dark, and I put the light on, to make sure that he was safe and well. He stirred a little, when I bent over and kissed him on the cheek.

It was only a bad dream, but the shock and pain of it were still in me, like an omen I could not afford to ignore. We were going to be separated very soon, and I found the thought of Piers dead almost comforting, because it was the one way I could be sure of not losing him back to the world. I looked down at the young body relaxed and warm in sleep. How would I ever manage to live without him, for whom I would have walked through fire?

Outside, the dawn was cold, grey and wet. The window was ajar, and the blankets had slid off, leaving us covered only by the sheet. Piers, in his sleep, put an arm round me, the heat of our bodies blended, and his breath was on my face. His tousled hair covered his closed eyes with their long lashes, his lips and ears were pink. He looked delicate, in sleep, and I knew that I had plucked a flower with a wilful, impious hand. I lay looking at him for a long time, unable to rid myself of the grim message of my dream, then got up, covering him over again, and walked across to the rainstreaked window. Outside, beyond the black outlines of the trees, a pinkness was trying to infuse the grey. The rain hissed down on foliage and grass, and I closed the window with a shiver and turned round, my heart troubled by something that I was only gradually beginning to understand: our relationship was too close for us to be able to see past it, we were becoming ingrown, and in no time at all the thing would blow up in our faces.

I suddenly felt alone and in need of advice. Piers could not help me, for he was as ensnared as I. What could a lad, who lay there sleeping like a baby, do to ease my conscience?

Outside, the rain fell harder, beating noisily on the window. Piers made a soft moaning sound in his sleep. My body began to freeze in the cold, damp air, until it was as chill and clammy as his had been, when I pulled it out of the sand. Perhaps, without my knowing it, without his knowing it, he had died indeed, and our love was no more than a hollow and hopeless thing.

I flung myself back into the bed, and he woke with a start to find me sobbing beside him.

'Roland, whatever's the matter?'

'Sorry, Piers. I just had one of my really bad nightmares.' Even if I could have found the words to tell him, they would only have cast more gloom over the day.

\*

He threw back his head and laughed. Piers, in the darkness, laughed at the bright, colourful form on the screen, where his image pushed a loaded wheelbarrow towards the camera, the sunlight making the sweat glisten on his bare torso. (Sand sticking to chill, white limbs, inert among the dunes). Boy and horse galloped down the beach and into the sea, and we caught our breath, as if the great gout of spray had struck us. (Spray, foaming up the grey strand, making my face smart, as my hands fought to uncover his body).

In his joy and enthusiasm for the pictures, he had momentarily forgotten me. I sat in silence by the whirring projector, looking at the screen as if it were a window on a past world, and still feeling numb inside, as though I had only recently come out of an operation.

He, thank goodness, seemed unworried by my quietness, though I knew that my occasional outbursts affected him, and *he* knew when to leave me alone. That morning, I had found him with a book, singing to himself. When I asked what it was, he smiled up at me and showed me the vocal score of Stravinsky's *Symphony of Psalms*. 'We're doing it at the end of term. I have to put in some work on it. I especially like this bit, near the end.' He began to sing, softly, the notes beautifully formed and assured. It was like God speaking aloud.

Tongue in cheek, I asked him whether he had ever felt he might want to become a priest, but he scornfully dismissed that idea. 'It might surprise you that some of them at Wharnley are really nasty pieces of work. They can be horrible to us, because they're just Philistines and they hate musicians.'

'Might you go in for a career in music, then?' I was fascinated by the notion that, like me, he might spend his life within the comforting world of creativity and beauty.

'I'd very much like to, but definitely not in church! I mean, I'd steer well clear of choirs. When you spend x-years pumping out Tallis and Sumsion and Stanford and all that crew... I'd be pleased to sing in something like, say, an opera.'

'Ever been to one?'

'My parents took me to Covent Garden once. It was *Aida*, and I loved every second of it.'

I told him that I had been commissioned to design an opera for Geneva.

'That's great. Is it by Verdi?'

'No. Benjamin Britten's working on *Death in Venice*, and the whole world is going to want it.'

'Ah yes, you told me about that. It's the one with the boy and the man. Will you do the costumes?'

'It's part of this commission, yes.'

'When you draw Tadzio, will you make him look like me?'

He wanted to know if I had ever met the composer myself. I told him I hadn't, though I did once briefly bump into Stravinsky. He was impressed by this name-dropping. 'How do I make a breakthrough into all that?'

'Firstly, you'll have to be quite a bit older,' I teased him. 'Knock about the world a bit, if you can, and pick up some contacts. And, of course, when your voice breaks, you'll have to find out whether you're a tenor or a bass.'

He wrinkled up his nose. 'It might be one of those poofy-sounding altos! Oops, sorry, Roland!'

I looked at him, and the same pinkness tinged his cheeks as I had seen in the Minster, when our relationship was still embryonic. Piers, you're beautiful, and I've already dared to intimate as much to you. Have you cottoned on, yet, to the significance of the all-too-obvious parallels with Tadzio? Am I paving the way to my own destruction, just as Aschenbach did?

I had taken the Stravinsky score from him, but my eyes did not even see the notes on the pages. End of term. Then Keatwells...

Having netted him so successfully at Whitsun, I wanted to ask what he would be doing in the summer holidays, but he had already mentioned that his parents would be back, and he would be staying with them at their flat near London. I tried hard not to take this as a rebuff.

The awareness that our time was running out bore down on us, our thoughts were already elsewhere, we were counting and recounting the hours, the minutes we had left. Time, which had seemed to amble along all the week, was gathering momentum now, moving too quickly, tarnishing the peace and harmony which we had at last managed to find together.

We spent more time entwined in one another, as if waiting in an air-raid shelter for the fury to break out over our heads.

'I feel I've become grown-up, with you,' he said. 'And you made things happen. You see, from the very first moment, I wanted things to happen...' It was his way of thanking me for helping him to mature.

But, like most of our talk during the last of our time together, it petered out, water trickling away into the sand. One was not allowed, after all, to get away with anything in this world. I had lived for Piers, loved him more dearly than any creature on earth, but it was all to no avail in the end. I was a fool to think that I could possess him, or he me. The closer I wanted to be with him, the further we seemed to be drifting away from one another, and I had to admit to myself that our affair had been doomed from the start. There had always been a time limit set on it, though we had both leaned over backwards to forget that fact, tried to ignore that he had brushed against me only briefly, like the mayfly, whose hours are numbered.

I fought the grief that threatened to overwhelm me and ruin the last precious moments with him, but inside I felt like a man who watches his loved one reach the end of an incurable disease. One waited for the end, and the waiting was surely far worse than the end itself.

In my desperation, I escaped from him, fled into the dunes and sobbed my heart out there, recalling his dream which he had related as we sat together in the early days in the tea-room: we were on the shore, he saw me in the distance and tried to get my attention, but I did not hear. A second later I was gone, the waves licking up the empty beach. Piers, suffocated in the sand tunnel, blood beneath his finger-nails. What had I done, that this should be the outcome? He had said more than once that I was a good man, so was this the reward for goodness? From the depths of my self-pity, I looked out on a world that was even blacker than usual. Too much happiness was wrong, ecstasy led only to misery and grief. I could see a soul going to its torment in the flames, powerless to do anything about it.

*

I woke him with a kiss, and 'Happy Birthday, *vieil homme!*'

He sat up, smiling at me, but then his face crumpled, and he burst into tears. 'Roland, we've got to go back today.' And then his grief turned to frenzied anger, and he shouted, kicked, swore, banging his head on the pillow. 'I'm not going back to that bloody place. I'm not!'

I took his hands in mine. 'Don't, Piers. It won't do any good, and it's not the best way to start your birthday.'

He calmed down, but his face remained streaked with tears. Why did life have to be so cruel, fussy and malevolent? If two beings loved each other, that should be enough, and the world should give them its blessing, never its curse.

'Look, I've got you something.' I took a small box and an envelope out of the drawer of the bedside table and handed them to him. His expression relaxed, and something of the old light came back into his eyes.

The card was one of my own designs: a galleon sailing across a foaming green sea, with a man on deck, looking through a telescope, and a boy at the helm. He grinned when he realised who had drawn it. 'Is that us?'

I managed an answering smile. 'Could be.'

When he saw the cuff-links, he was even more delighted. 'I've never had anything made of gold before.'

It was as if I had given him an ancient, valuable treasure. 'I was afraid you might find them banal – an uncle's gift to his favourite nephew.'

'They're not the slightest bit banal, and you aren't my uncle, either!' He got out of bed, went over to our wardrobe, and came back with a packet about the same size and shape as the one I had given him. 'It's a thank-you for having had me to stay, but it's something else, too.' He climbed back on the bed and sat on the pillow, with his legs crossed and eyes unusually bright.

My fingers trembled as I opened the box. It was a ring, a plain metal ring.

'Look inside it,' he said huskily, and I held it up to my eye. Two words were engraved on the inner face of it, and I had to twist it about until the light caught them: "Roland-Piers". I lowered it again, struggling with my emotions. 'It's a wonderful present.'

'People abroad have their names engraved on them, don't they?'

'But you shouldn't have spent all your money on me.'

'I wanted to. It's not gold, I'm afraid, and in any case you shouldn't have bought me the cuff-links, but I'm glad you did.'

The burden on my heart had lifted a little. He took my hand, looking for the ring finger. 'Have you any other rings, Roland?'

'No.' I had recently suppressed them for, in our relationship, Barry, Jonathan and Fiona played no part. They were ghosts now, and we had exorcised them.

Piers put the ring on my finger and we kissed, as if to seal the bond.

'We'll still see each other,' I said, with my arm round his shoulder, 'just as we used to, before we came here.' Five weeks of meetings at the tea-shop and in the car lay before us.

'We'll come back here too, won't we, Roland?'

'Of course we will.' Though a little warning voice was urging me not to make promises I did not intend to keep.

'And when I move on to Keatwells, I'll still be able to come and see you, won't I?' He was banking on the fact that I would soon be owner of "Stella Maris".

I could not resist breaking across our litany of mutual reassurance by teasing him a little. 'You may not want me any more when you're at your grown-up public school!'

'Oh Roland, I could never forget you. I'd always want to come back to you. Perhaps, when I'm old enough, I'll be able to come for a very long time.'

Another painful thought struck me. I had tried to encourage him to obey the pressures of society, and to think of marriage - *real* marriage - as a natural path for the future, but had I really drawn him into my own camp, so that he would later go with men instead? For the time being, though he was just entering his teens, he was still a child in many ways, who could be fobbed off with vague promises. 'Yes, Piers, that would be nice.'

But he was not satisfied with that! 'Please say I can come back. We *are* married now, aren't we? I've given you a ring to prove it. It's not just a game. Please, Roland, please.'

He was near to tears again, and I could not resist him when he was like this. 'You know I love you and always will, and I swear I'll keep a place for you, wherever I am.'

'Swear it on the ring.' He was panting, in his distress.

I kissed the ring which he had put on my finger and swore, as he had asked me to do. The Wagnerian overtones of this did not escape me.

In the lovemaking that followed, easily and naturally, he was more excited and passionate than I had ever known before, even in our greatest moments together. As if inspired, and ablaze with immense fervour, he seemed to be struggling with soul and body to encompass me. Because we were so soon to be parted, I could only humour him, let him have his way, hoping that it would not harm him. He suddenly sat up and looked at me, eyes burning. 'Come inside me, Roland. It's all right. We are *are* married.'

I was tempted almost beyond what anyone could bear. He was handing himself to me, on a plate, already rolling over on to his stomach. As I usually did, last thing at night before we went to sleep, I put my hand down on one of his buttocks, and quietly rubbed his back, to and fro, feeling the warm softness of him, the cherubic young flesh which he was so desperate to bestow on me for any use I chose.

He took this to be a gentle refusal on my part, not realising why my own reaction was calmer now, almost dispassionate, for my dark premonition was growing all the time.

The man came from the farm later in the morning, to collect the horse. Sunday church bells and newspapers reminded us that he had to be back in school after tea today. We walked about outside, arm-in-arm, recalling happy moments spent in the orchard or paddock. Finally, we entered the dunes. It was a hot day, and the whiteness of the sand glared at us, the blue of the sky merging with that of the sea.

Not wishing to upset us both, I had not told him of my nightmare about the sand tunnel. We stripped off and, at his behest, swam a race. When we were a good distance from land, he called, 'Roland, where were you, the year I was born?'

He came splashing over to me, and we lay floating, side by side.

'Oh, I would have been in Paris, just about to return to London.'

'What were you doing out there?' He made Paris sound as if it was in the Far East!

'I'd finished my Art training, in both places, and I was about to start to scratch a living.' Barry came on the scene a few months later.

'So, which year were you born in?'

'I don't think I'd better say. It was before the war.'

Forgetting where he was, Piers tried to sit up, and sank. 'Nineteen-thirty something? he spluttered.

'The year of the Berlin Olympics. Adolf Hitler and all that.'

'Christ! I don't know that date.'

I told him.

'Then,' he said, rolling over on to his stomach and executing a lazy breast-stroke, 'Hitler or no, it was the best year of all! D'you remember I once told you I thought you might be a German? Anyhow, I've decided to do German, if I can, at my next school – with French, of course.'

If he had the impression that I wasn't truly English any more, he put his finger on it exactly.

*

Looking into the steaming casserole and seeing pieces of meat among the carrots, mushrooms and potatoes, he pulled a face. 'This is the last decent meal I shall get, before going back to pig-swill.'

'Not quite the last.' But I did not elaborate, because the tea was to be a surprise. I poured him a small glass of Main wine, making him exhilarated and quite dotty, and bringing some welcome laughter to chase away our earlier intense and mournful feelings.

When we had washed up, and were sitting down with a cup of very black coffee, he looked at me with eyes that were suddenly sober. 'Roland…'

I knew the tone, knew it heralded something which would strike at me, deep inside.

'How will I manage, about sex, I mean? I've become so used to doing it with you, that when I'm on my own again…'

I put an arm round his shoulder. 'How was it, before we came together, you and I?'

He tipped his head from one side to the other. 'Little game, sometimes, just for comfort, you see. But now *sometimes* isn't enough. Wouldn't it be unfaithful to you, after all that we've..?'

'Piers, just don't worry about it. Between us, it was love. What you do alone doesn't count.'

'I know. But what about you?'

I do not blush often, but he had caught me, this time. 'Whatever happens, I shall be thinking of you.'

'And I'll think of you too,' he said, brightening up, 'which will make it more like proper love, won't it?'

'Like sending a message, Piers, even if it doesn't actually reach the other person.'

He took my hand and fingered the ring which he had given me. 'I swear I won't do it with anyone else but you,' he said solemnly.

In my relief, I kissed his hair. Although we were momentarily happy again, I felt the tears near the surface. Whatever happened to our love from now on, it would never be the same again, for a shaft had penetrated its heart.

'You look so sad, Roland.'

I forced a smile. 'It's the wine. I shouldn't drink it, it always depresses me.'

He hugged me. 'Don't be sad. Let's be happy for the last few hours.'

I looked at him. 'Don't speak as if we won't meet again. I couldn't bear that.' Now I was being the faint-heart.

'I didn't mean it like that.' He put his cheek against mine.

We went down to the beach, but not to swim. Instead, we walked far along by the water's edge, mostly in silence. Neither of us was relaxed, and I knew that we would not be, until I had delivered him to his school and driven away again.

We sat down in the dunes, he put his head in my lap and, like a puppy, suddenly fell asleep. I did not have the heart to disturb him, and why should I? Where Tadzio loitered by the water's edge, Piers' lover had his boy cosily with him. My gloominess began to lift, as I thought of how the future might shape up for us, however short-term it might be. *We* were not going to be severed by death.

\*

The things for the tea came out of their various hiding-places and on to the low table in the lounge, which was less formal than the dining-room. I let him help me carry the ingredients through – trifle, biscuits, sandwiches and tea – and was relieved to see his rising excitement. At last, when everything was ready, I closed the curtains and went out alone into the kitchen. On my return, he gave a whoop of delight. I put the cake down in the centre of the table, and the candles flickered gently. Thirteen of them, illuminating the birthday message: "Love to Piers".

'That's really great, Roland. The last time I had a birthday cake was...' He frowned and shook his head. 'Dunno. Must have been when I was five or six.'

'I was afraid you'd find it too young for you.'

But he did not, and we sat down to the meal in high spirits. For a few precious minutes we took tea together, with all the hope, joy and companionship that we had enjoyed in the tea-shop, he the fresh, delightful schoolboy, and I the awkward but persistent suitor. I felt as though Piers and I had been sharing our lives since the world began, and I shrank from the thought that our paths would ever diverge, his to the enveloping world of a new school, mine to a future of solitude and possible remorse.

When, shortly afterwards, I opened the curtains and pressed the button to close the big window, it was like a prison door sliding shut, leaving a world of colour, gaiety and freedom on the far side. He carried his case out to the Mercedes and stood, looking back at the cottage. It was as if I saw Barry's ghost. Drawing level with him, I saw that he too was fighting back the tears, and I put my hand on his shoulder.

'I don't want to go back,' he said quickly, in a taut voice. 'Why can't you take me somewhere else? Why can't we go to Switzerland, or - ?'

'If I did that, they would catch up with us, and the consequences would be severe. We've got to be very careful not to give each other away. Not a word about our time spent here.'

I was turning it into something furtive and shameful, and feared that he might start to take a very different view of our affair, which had been, to my mind, pure and holy till now. 'The world doesn't understand. What we regard as good and beautiful, for us, is breaking the law in other men's eyes.'

'Oh Christ.' He looked at me in consternation. 'But I don't care, because it wasn't one of those abduction things, was it? I don't see how it could be wrong – not with you.'

His spiritedness should have consoled me. I knew that, in my craven desire to get him to keep quiet about our stay together, I had spoilt the end of it.

The afternoon sunshine beat at us through the windscreen, blinding and hot. Tears were pouring down his cheeks now. 'I swear that I shan't tell anyone. And we will meet again very soon. We aren't finished, are we?' He was struggling to speak through the sobs, Piers the teenager momentarily eclipsed, and I had a young boy beside me who needed a fatherly shoulder to cry on. I stopped the car and cuddled him to me.

'Piers, I don't regret a single second of my time with you. I love you and I always shall, and nothing can ever alter that. Do you think that I could live without the prospect of seeing you again? I need that hope to feed on. Don't ever forget that. You may not understand it fully yet, but you will, before many years have passed.' When he is twenty-one, I shall be forty-three and no longer to his taste. I had told him to head back to the world with its starchy conventions, but at the same time I wanted him for myself.

As if reading my thoughts, he looked up and said, 'I'll never forget you, and I'll never stop loving you, even if I get married one day, like you said.' I could ask for no more comforting message from him than this and, by the time the Minster towers appeared on the skyline, growing in stature as we sped onward towards them, the leaden feeling inside me was already giving way to a feeling of fresh hope.

## V.

In the next few days, as the vacuum inside me slowly filled again, I could see the irony of it: our parting promised to restore to us the edge which our unconventional relationship had begun to lose during the stay at the cottage. Total freedom to do and say whatever we wanted, to be ourselves, had threatened to kill the affair stone dead. It needed the dash of danger, of adventure, of furtive meetings at night, of looks and words secretly exchanged in public – above all, it needed to be thoroughly illicit, in order to succeed.

We were back in our original setting, but neither could say he was unscathed, unchanged by what had just happened to us. We both carried, within, an intimate knowledge of the other, we had trodden forbidden ground and eaten forbidden fruit. Before we met, I had quite forgotten what it was like, to be desired by another.

Now I was elated again, impatient, ready to seize every opportunity, however small or tantalising, to see him, to speak to him, to tell him of the love that burnt me up with new flames. And, knowing my Piers, I was perfectly sure that he was feeling the same about me.

Whenever I looked at the ring which he had put on my finger, I saw *his* fingers which, like those of a young and inquisitive child, had sought out the landscape of my body. He had been like a baby that wants to know everything, finding out all things for himself. He was the leader in these games, and I gladly went where he took me, even if it meant sounding the depths as well. At moments like this, my guilty feelings obligingly melted away.

My lodging windows were flung open, not only to the summer (which had now burst in upon the town with vigour and abandon) but also to the bell-notes of the great church, high on its hill above, where, at every service, I sat opposite him in my stall, jubilant at the converse of our eyes. We knew, we shared, we experienced, and I was in paradise once more, where time seemed unimportant, any hastiness on our part irrelevant now.

The Minster, that magical forest, welcomed me back as a place fit to shelter our love, as if the blocks of ancient masonry, the soaring pillars and stained glass windows, the very paving-stones even, were a fertile seed-bed, deprived of which the plant would perish. Jove looked down on us from above. 'Impudent,' he said, 'but not beyond the pale.' For me at least, all was now in flux, the Minster was losing its Christian meaning, and becoming instead a kind of Greek temple in which the man-boy connection could be glorified without any feeling of shame.

My thoughts were constantly occupied with Piers, devising ways in which we could continue to meet in private. My zeal however continued to be tempered by concern as to how his future life might be affected by having known me. An answer came, one sultry, thundery night, when, as heavy raindrops spattered the warm roofs and pavements, I woke out of a dream to find myself standing at the window of my bedroom, convinced that tears were wetting my face: his tears.

It had begun at the Reception, where I had been making a speech, complimenting him upon his choice of bride, while indicating quite clearly that he and I were the close ones, and would always be so. My eyes had strayed to the two sets of parents. His, in dirty dungarees and caps, the grime of eastern churches still upon them, lapped up my every word with obvious approval. *Hers,* in immaculate morning dress and gown, smiled at my empty tributes to their daughter, 'this jewel of loveliness', but looked puzzled when I mentioned Piers as 'a young man for whom I have had a tender affection for some time now.'

He, in all this, did not take his eyes from me for one second, and I knew exactly what that expression conveyed: 'There, I've done it, because you made me. But don't fear: it won't change anything between *us.* '

I closed the window, and let the big warm drops patter down it. How had the dream ended? After the honeymoon, he had returned to me, distraught, banished and, as I held him in my arms, begging me to release him from a duty which brought him no joy, - as though Barry or Jonathan came knocking at my door. With his tears warm on my cheek, I had woken up, ridden with a strange mixture of triumph and remorse.

This triggered the memory of another occasion, at the cottage, when the rain beat down outside, while I watched the coming of a dawn of doubt and shame. Lord, *what had I taught him?* I went hot and cold at the thought, I tried to find a consoling solution to the problem, but words like "abducted" and "perverted" and "paederast" flashed across my consciousness like a sniper's bullets.

I sought comfort in re-reading Plutarch's *Dialogues*, and Lucian's *Affairs of the Heart*, dwelling upon the references to pleasures with boys, and finding plenty of justification for what Piers and I had undertaken together. But then a cold sobriety returned. I knew I had acted recklessly, but hadn't Piers egged me on in an affair which he, at least, had regarded as a kind of 'marriage' from the very start? If I doubted that, the ring on my finger was a constant and nagging reminder. "Those whom God has joined, let no man put asunder". And I knew that, for him, there was still some unfinished business to be completed. *Anything.* For all my attempts at self-delusion, we were both back in the world now, which was ready, any moment, to tear us apart.

\*

A week or so after our return to town, I sat with him in the tea-room. He was bright-eyed as always, and we were both keyed up merely by this simple contact with each other, and by the secret we shared. I was pleased that life had taken on a new purpose for him, but concerned by his keenness to push our newly-created adventure further along its way, for there was now only one direction that it could possibly go from here.

As if reading my thoughts, he asked if we could return to the cottage tonight and, when I shook my head, quickly added, 'I'm sure there's a tramp or somebody around, over there. He might break in and sleep in one of the beds.'

He must have known that I would see through this gauche excuse but, to humour him, judged it wiser to suggest that tomorrow, being Friday, might be a better day. He could obtain an *exeat* for the weekend.

But his face fell. 'We've got a match on Saturday, and I shan't be able to get out of nets practice tomorrow evening. Can't we just go out *somewhere* tonight, then? There are… things I want to say to you that I can't say here.' He had raised his voice, and I had to put a warning hand on his wrist.

'Get out of school as usual at ten,' I said quietly, 'and I'll be waiting.'

He looked at his watch and was about to get up. 'Oh Christ!'

'What's the matter?'

'That man, over by the window, on his own. It's bloody Hutters. You know, I told you about him. I think he's seen us.'

'Just stay right where you are, Piers. Maybe he'll go away.' There was a cold sensation at the back of my neck.

'Bet he doesn't. He's vicious, he doesn't like me, because... I wouldn't go up to the loft with him for organ lessons.' He had gone pink.

I pondered this revelation for a moment. 'Hang on here. I'll pay the bill and come back.'

Feeling sick in the pit of my stomach, I went to the till, gave our young waitress some money, and looked cautiously round. There was a short, balding man, older than I, occupying a table near the window, and studying the enormous cream tea which had just been placed in front of him. It would be impossible for anyone making for the front door to pass him without being noticed.

I quietly said to the waitress, 'Is there another way out of here? Someone I really don't want to bump into...'

She looked at me in surprise. I pressed some more coins into her hand and, taking my meaning, she gave me a quick shy smile and said, 'If you go down the passage past the toilet at the back, you come out in an alley-way. It leads back to the street.'

I thanked her, returned to our table, gave Piers some rapid instructions and covered his hasty departure by the rear exit. I did not think that the man in the window had seen us. What we had just done might well chime in with Piers' idea of our relationship as an on-going escapade, but I was going to have to block his increasingly risky suggestions, and soon. At least his cricket match would give me some respite. I might even go and watch it.

\*

He came jauntly out of the alley-way and climbed into the car. Black polo neck, jeans, the same old expression of tenseness and mischief in his lovely face. My heart rose and sank again.

'I want you to take me to "Stella" now, he said quietly, but with a steely firmness. 'We don't know when we'll get the next chance.'

I didn't have the slightest intention of doing what he asked, because it would only lead to things which I must now resist. When he realised that I was heading to the spot by the river where we had gone on our first trip out, he demanded to know why, with a note of alarm in his voice and a light in his eye which I had seen, and been disturbed by, before.

'There really isn't time to get to the cottage and back tonight,' I said, trying to summon up the courage which the glass of red wine should have given me. My pulses had started racing as soon as I set eyes on him tonight. He was so boyish, fresh, delightful and utterly desirable, and I wanted him as desperately as he wanted me – in *that* way. To take him to the cottage and allow that to happen would destroy us both for ever. Oh Piers, I have to get rid of you – and quickly!

It was still daylight when I pulled up at the end of the lane leading to the river. Before I knew what was happening, he leant across, put a strong arm round my shoulders and clamped his lips to mine. It was a shock assault, with his tongue seeking passage between my lips, and I had to fight to push him back, to stop what he had begun, before it reached the point where a halt could no longer be called.

He recoiled with a look that stung me to the soul. 'Roland, whatever's wrong?' In all our many encounters at the cottage, I had guided him, restrained him, but never repulsed him.

I took a deep breath. 'I want to talk to you, Piers.' It was as though we were about to embark on an almighty row.

The tears were already welling up in his eyes, a sure sign that I was handling it badly. 'You do still love me, don't you, Roland?'

It was my turn to put an arm round his shoulder, and he beat his head against me, breaking out into a torrent of weeping and incoherent words. The sobs racked him, as though he were a very small boy overcome by an uncontrollable grief because he could not understand why a favourite toy was being withheld.

'You know I love you, Piers. Steady does it, now.'

'I've been… saving myself for you,' he at last managed to blurt out.

'Don't think I don't appreciate that,' I said, gently stroking his hair. 'The last thing I want is to hurt you, but I really must talk with you. You see, my love for you is as strong as yours for me, but there's something blocking the way. I just don't know if I'm right for you, in the end. It's not the same out here, is it, when we're both back in the world again? It's exciting, but it's really very dangerous. I don't want you to get into any kind of trouble.' Liar that I am!

He sat up, looking at me with eyes that seemed to speak of betrayal, and my mouth went dry. Had he divined my true thoughts? His tears came again, but he would not let me comfort him this time. He edged back to his own side, rocking and trembling, his hands to his eyes, his mouth distorted like a rubber band.

'Piers, listen. You must get help.'

He did not seem to hear. Still, his body was convulsed with sobs, and I had to fight my own emotions as well.

'You must find someone else, to discuss it with and get advice. I can't help you in this. Look at the effect I'm having on you now.'

At last, he lowered his hands and stared at me. I turned my face away to the river, unable to bear the sight of him like that, for it made me as desolate and helpless as he was.

'You need someone apart from me. Isn't there a priest you could go to?'

He muttered something unintelligible.

A sense of objectivity had begun to grow in me, and I was already feeling a little easier. 'Don't you see that we've reached a point where we are too ingrown? We need to see our relationship through another's eyes.'

'That's not what you said before. You said not to breathe a word about it to anyone else. And now you're changing it all. I don't understand, Roland, and I don't understand you any more. You told me only a minute ago that you loved me, and now... I thought I could trust you. I don't *need* to talk to anyone else, when I've got you.'

I never failed to be surprised by the adult way in which he sometimes spoke. It was a man, even more mature than Barry or Jonathan, with whom I kept company at these moments, not a youth called Piers. He was calmer now, though he still sat at a distance from me.

'Will you do it, just for me?' I said, quietly but earnestly.

To my relief, he nodded. 'If that's what you want.' He said it as if to humour me, but I did not care.

'And you will tell him about us, won't you?'

'Everything?' His eyes were wide.

'Dwell more on the emotional side of it. And be sure to keep back my identity, and the address of the cottage.' Or we shall both be in the soup.

'D'you really mean I'm to talk about our lovemaking?' It was a word I must have used to him at some point. Now it rebounded, and struck me.

'It won't be easy, Piers, but it'll clear the air. Then you can come and tell me what was said.'

He evidently thought that all this was just a whim of mine. As we drove back, he was quiet. I knew that he had expected us to make love in the car, if not at the cottage, and I knew that he was bitterly disappointed. So was I, but I hid it, and filled the void by planning our next meeting. In a few days, he would have had a chance to seek out a confessor, and could then report back to me.

It was already dark when we parked by the Minster. 'Choose someone understanding and discreet, if possible,' I said, 'and don't go into details about your method of getting out at night.'

When it came to the moment to kiss him goodbye, I gripped him tightly in my arms, rubbing my head against his, feeling his smooth warm face against mine, and finally tasting his fresh moist lips, his teeth, the dark and secret corners of his mouth. We kissed with fervent desire, as if it was all over, now. He was breathless, marvellous and acquiescent. He made no advances, but let me spend my fund of fire and zeal on him. At last, when my heart was pounding, I gave him a little push. 'God bless, Piers.'

'God bless, Roland.' It was almost choked by a sob.

A passing car's headlamps lit up his figure for a second. He looked big, an adolescent already, not a boy any more, and I felt a rush of pride at the thought that this was my doing. Then he was gone, and I waited on tenterhooks for his signal. But whether he forgot to flash his light, or something had gone wrong, no signal came. I waited for ten minutes, and then drove slowly away.

*

The bellringers had long since finished their Saturday evening practice, and now the Minster clock, striking quarter past ten, increased my feeling of disquiet: he had not made the rendezvous, and it was not like him. I could not believe that he would stay away voluntarily, so had he been discovered? Had that sub-organist man ratted on us? Or had Piers duly made his confession, and been punished for his pains?

At first, like someone awaiting a dear friend whose return from a solo mountain climb was overdue, I tried every rational argument that I could muster: Piers had not judged it safe to make his usual escape into the cloisters, tonight; or perhaps he had mislaid the key and didn't dare to walk out through the front door of the school.

It was mild, the last light was dying away in the sky, and I was sitting with the window of the car wound down, when I heard footsteps coming up from behind (not Piers' light boyish tread, but something more deliberate, more military even), and found a helmeted head looking in at me.

'May I inquire why you are waiting here, sir?'

I nearly jumped out of my skin, to find a policeman at my elbow. Being well used to awkward gendarmes, I decided to brazen it out. 'Is it illegal to park here? I'm not on a yellow line or something, am I?'

The policeman was very young and, I assumed, new to the job. Evidently realising that he was dealing neither with a hardened criminal nor a foreigner, he adopted a more respectful tone. 'It's just that we have to check up now and then on parked cars, sir. And you have got Swiss plates. May I see your passport?'

'Look, I'm British, and I'm just waiting here for somebody...'

'Nonetheless, sir, if you wouldn't mind,' he said, and put out his hand. 'Oh yes, and the driving licence and car docs.'

I opened the glove compartment and gave him the papers, which he looked at carefully with the aid of a torch. I was praying that Piers would not suddenly appear and, seeing a policeman interrogating me, flee from the scene.

'Everything in order, sir. Sorry to have troubled you.' There was just a suggestion of disappointment in the constable's voice, perhaps because he had not chanced upon some member of the international mafia. He gave me a self-conscious nod, straightened up and continued on his beat. As I watched his uniformed figure striding along the street in front, a number of distressing thoughts went through my head. The clock chimed again.

Shivering now, despite myself, I got out of the car, and looked up at Piers' window. If he was still in school, his light would surely be on, and he would be in there. Maybe I could somehow attract his attention. But the window was in darkness, a fact which I could not help taking as a rejection.

I felt so useless not to be able to get in touch with him, especially as it now mattered to me more than anything in the world to see him, speak to him, share some precious moments of closeness with him, and be reassured that there was no problem clouding our happiness together. But then I was reminded of the task I had given him. I hadn't meant to send him to his doom, *or had I?* Wasn't it merely the awareness of our approaching perdition, that night, that made me say the first thing that occurred to me? If he was no longer a free agent, could it really be all my own doing?

To keep a lower profile, I re-parked the car out of sight down a side-street and returned on foot to our rendezvous point, where I remained glued to the spot for an endless hour and a half (measured out in mocking bell-notes), hoping that something harmless would have detained him and that, at any time, his dear form would detach itself from the shadows, and come to me.

In the end, I drove back to my depressing rooms in the lower town. I was tempted to ring up the school, posing as a relative bringing urgent news, and ask to speak to him. But school switchboards were not manned by secretaries at such an hour as this – and I did not wish to risk being answered by the Headmaster or his Deputy, both of whom had been given a scornful thumbnail sketch by Piers during an earlier tea-shop session, light-years ago, before we had properly found each other...

Looking the obvious solution in the face helped to ease my gloom somewhat: if Piers could not come to me, I, by continuing to attend all the services at which the boys sang, would soon establish, by signs or looks, what was afoot. As always, he would see me, look at me, and understand. It would surely be a simple matter to intercept him and make a new rendezvous.

*

I sat in the gloom, the excitement of the early days within me replaced by a new and bewildering claustrophobia. The ancient wood of the stalls enclosed me, but their familiar odour did not comfort me any more. I was back at the edge of the arena once again, but no longer safely anonymous. Everything around me today pointed up a massive discrepancy between the road which Piers and I had taken together, and what the unfeeling, stuffy world's opinion would be, if it knew.

They came filing solemnly through the narrow archway, as if about to attend an execution. My heart almost burst when I saw him, not my Piers in Bermuda shorts, nor my boy naked, but a chorister in hooded cope again, formal and impersonal, at the front of the procession as always. I stood and watched him pass. A ray of sunlight descended between us and, as the boy passed behind it, his form became, for a brief moment, ethereal and intangible. *I always brought him back safe and sound, so I cannot be an abductor.*

The Evensong began. I sat and stared, knowing all the many moments at which he would look at me, and waiting with anticipation for the first. The sunlight slowly moved across and lit up that face so dear to me. When he sang, it seemed to be without his usual attack and verve, and his eyes no longer travelled calmly along the tiers of stalls on the opposite side – where I was sitting – but remained cast downward, either at his book or, when he was sitting, at his knees. It was as if nothing had ever happened between us, as if we were complete strangers, as if I did not even exist.

The Choir bore down upon me like a vast rock prison or tomb even. The music, reduced to empty, arid chanting, failed to move me. I wanted to leave this place for good, for there no longer seemed to be anything to keep me here.

The Old Testament lesson talked of the sinful cities of the plain, and their destruction by an angry God. *I did not penetrate him, I am not a Sodomite.* (Though, on that last evening together, something was very much in the air, and we both knew it…)

At length, to my great relief, it is over, and they process out, he looking neither to right nor left. Broken in spirit, I force myself to take up position in the cloister by the door leading into the school, where he can hardly avoid the gaze of a man who will even risk speaking to him, as the twenty boys return. And, being my beloved, he will respond as always.

The door bangs on the far side, where he first smiled at me, and gave me hope. They come along quickly, in a tight bunch, (the fairhaired one called Fillingham scanning me briefly with his brown eyes), and pass on. Bringing up the rear with the tall, grey-haired priest whom I have seen before, is Piers, so my hope of accosting him is dashed. There is indeed a pallor, a tension even, in his face, as he steps silently along, almost sullenly, a prisoner with his gaoler. *Is this the man who stole him from me?*

I look at my boy, but he keeps his eyes averted, though he knows very well that I am standing here, for a flush rises in his cheek as he approaches the open door and is lost to sight. Whether he found my presence embarrassing or not, I do not care. What tortures me so is the sight of my beloved one, so unresponsive, so terribly correct, crestfallen even. *What has that man done to him?* Whatever it might be, it must be far worse than any experience he ever shared with me. While we were together, he was supremely happy and fulfilled.

Slowly, I walked away down the alley along which he had come to my car at night, and suddenly I knew why he had not acknowledged me: it would have given away his lover's identity to the people who now guarded him.

In my impatience, I nearly buttonholed another boy from the school, whom I saw in the town, to get him to take a message from me, but feared it might compromise both of them. My chief concern in all this was that, (having been caught trying to leave the school, or nabbed when he left my car to return there), he would have been interrogated by his teachers until they had teased out every last detail of our precious relationship, and turned him against me. But surely he was made of sterner stuff than that, he wouldn't break down under pressure? It was clear, thank God, that he would not reveal my identity to them.

At first, I found a wicked grain of comfort in the notion that he was afflicted as much as I was over this, and hoped that, in his silent and solitary moments, I would often be in his thoughts. But then it distressed me that my own clumsiness and cowardice might be the cause of his suffering, for there was no other word to describe the state he was evidently now in.

*

Canon Byatt-Woods switched on the light, gestured to him to enter, and shut the door. 'I deemed it better to speak to you in here, where we should not be interrupted.'

The library was lined with shelves bearing ancient volumes bound in dark leather, exuding the Wharnley smell of dust and decay. The priest motioned him to sit on a chair in front of a huge table, while he took his place on another, at right angles.

'So, Moriston, I will come straight to the point: late yesterday evening, you were discovered by the Duty Master, arriving at school well after lights out, and without permission to be out. You had in your hand a key to the door leading into the cloisters. I say "*a* key", because it transpires that the normal one was in place on its hook in the Secretary's office. This one,' and he placed a Yale key on the table in front of them, 'is quite clearly a duplicate. How did it come to be in your possession? Did you get it made?'

But the boy preserved a sullen, defensive silence.

'Moriston, you are a senior boy and in a position of trust here, but you are still bound by the rules of the school, which are framed to protect all you boys from possible harm. You understand and accept that much, I take it?'

This time, the boy gave a faint nod.

'I expect an explanation from you,' said the priest, leaning forward and tapping the key, 'and I don't intend to be all night about it.'

'I'm sorry, sir, but I can't tell you,' said the boy, crimson-faced.

'Oh but I think you can,' said Byatt-Woods, with a hard edge to his voice now. 'There is too much at stake, here. You have a place at Keatwells, have you not? It could well be that you will lose that, if you do not give me the information I require. I only have to lift the telephone and speak to the headmaster there, and your chances are in ruins.'

'But why, sir?' The boy choked on his question, and there were tears in his eyes.

'Why? Because you have behaved in a deceitful and possibly dangerous fashion, and you have forfeited our trust in you. I should have thought that was reason enough.'

The boy sat there, his hands clamped together, slowly shaking his head. 'It isn't what you think, not at all. It's something rather wonderful, in fact.'

Canon Byatt-Woods put the shining brass key away in his pocket, and folded his arms. 'Wonderful? Whatever do you mean by that?'

'You see, I met this man.' The words came blurting out just like that. Roland had told him to go and talk to someone. He hadn't explained what to do, if that someone started it and waded straight in. 'He invited me to go and stay at his cottage, by the sea.'

'How and where did you meet him? Who is he? Where is he now? When was this? I want answers.' The priest stopped his machine-gun attack and was looking grimly at him again.

Moriston was dazed. He could only reply to the last bit of the volley. 'Over the Whit half-term hol, sir.' He thought of Mother's letter agreeing to his going off with Roland, but it was based on lies he had told her, and in any case it had Roland's name in it. He had lost the initiative already and his courage was ebbing away.

'All right, just recently, then. And what did you do at his cottage *by the sea?*'

The boy's face had frozen. He had no idea what might be coming next. There wasn't even a chance to put together some clever lies. 'We went swimming, and I helped with the gardening.' His throat was strangled, and the words 'Did some riding' were virtually inaudible.

'And the two of you got the key made, so that you could come and go as you pleased during term-time, when school was in session? You had been to see this man last night, when Mr Thorpe intercepted you?'

It was no good. He could only capitulate, back away, get out of it somehow. All that mattered now was to protect Roland, if that was still possible. He'd said far too much, as it was.

'This man… Was he close to you?'

The boy nodded, involuntarily.

'A friend of your family, perhaps?'

A shake of the head. The tears were beginning to course down his cheeks now. He sat there, woebegone, defenceless, no match at all for his interlocutor.

'And… his name. Tell me that.'

There was a silence which never seemed to end.

'Did you let him touch you and did he get you to touch him? I think you know what I mean.' The voice was quiet, but there was a razor sharpness to it. A bell sounded, far away.

He swallowed hard, fighting the tears. 'We were – we are – very good friends.' He was as if paralysed, for a whole new dimension was being thrust upon him now.

'You have not properly answered my question. So, let me put it differently: *did you go to bed together?*'

Roland and he had always been truthful. To do anything else would make their loving partnership go sour. He took a very deep breath. 'It wasn't - .'

' – wasn't anything *wrong*, Moriston?'

Knowing it was hopeless, he shook his head and rested his palms on the cool wood of the table in front of him. When he took them away, they left smudgy prints which gradually disappeared, reminding him of fingerprints, police and prison.

'Tell me this, then. How do you account for the tub of Vaseline found in your pocket?'

The boy jumped, as if he had been shot. 'Why… it was just that I had a sore place on my foot.'

'And you took it from the medicine chest without asking Matron?' Byatt-Woods' face was flushed now. 'Did you not know what might happen, after all the warnings we have given about never talking to strangers, and certainly not going with them?'

A cowardly caution stayed the boy's tongue. He knew that, if he did nothing to defend Roland, he would be betraying him. All he could stammer was, 'He's kind and loving. He isn't a monster.' He rummaged in his pocket for the clean handkerchief he'd put there, just in case.

'It shocks me,' said the Canon, 'that one of our boys, from a Christian setting such as this, should go off the rails so badly. Have you quite forgotten what sin is?'

The boy could restrain his sobs no longer. They shook his body, echoing round the dry gloomy space where they sat.

'You realise that we have to know what he did to you, Moriston. Moral harm is serious, but physical harm can be even more damaging. So, out with it now.'

But he could only drum his clenched fists on the table.

'If you are to save yourself, you must tell me his name.'

The boy ceased the drumming and sat still now, occasionally convulsed with a deep sob like a hiccup.

'He isn't worth shielding, Moriston.'

'You… would only give it to the police.' In his fear and anguish, his voice had pitched itself high, like that of one of the little boys.

'Ah, so you admit that something happened which you knew was against the law. Your words prove that you have done wrong.'

Somewhere outside the window, two crows were having an argument. Otherwise, except for the boy's sniffing, the vast gloomy library was as quiet as a tomb.

'I assume that you have another rendezvous with him planned, yes? Well, let me tell you this: he has had what he wanted from you, and now he will drop you. To continue seeing you would be too dangerous for him. You'll see, he will disappear from the scene.'

Amid his upset, he was aware that the Canon was trying to edge him towards making a revelation which would threaten Roland and himself. He noisily blew his nose.

'Let me assure you that you will *not* be seeing him again. He won't dare to show his face in the Minster.' The priest was staring hard at the boy, obviously expecting a retort. 'And now I must ask you one or two more things. We know how you contrived to come and go at will. Did the arrangement with the spare key commence prior to Whitsun?'

But caution won again, and the boy merely gazed ahead in silence.

'Your actions will lead to a necessary tightening up of our security. The other boys, thanks to you, will also lose something of their freedom. I shall tell you tomorrow what punishment I propose to deal out to you for this outrageous and quite unacceptable behaviour on your part... Tell me, Moriston, when your parents propose to come back to England. Will they be at home when term ends?'

'They'll be back at the flat the same day,' he said leadenly. 'Are you going to tell them about..?'

The priest looked at him and, for the first time, hesitated. 'We shall of course keep you under close supervision until then. I think you are old enough to make your own decision about what to say and what not to. It would be better not to upset them.'

'Thank you, sir. What about Keatwells?' He raised his wet face and managed to look Byatt-Woods in the eye.

'I shall have to ponder that also. You have certainly let this school down badly – very badly indeed – as well as yourself.'

The clock chimed again outside. The evening was closing in. The boy sat and shivered.

'I am going to take you out of the power of this wicked person,' said the priest. 'We will finish with a prayer. Close your eyes, put your hands together and say with me: *Our Father...*'

He led off in his dry, confident altar voice, the boy limped on behind, almost suffocating on the phrase "and lead us not into temptation", and only just whispering the final "amen". It was as if he had been made to pronounce a sentence over his lover. He looked up. 'Sir, will you say a prayer for him?'

'Certainly not,' snapped the priest.

At this, all his defences broken, Piers Moriston flew into a rage. 'Then I don't give a fig for all your so-called Christianity! It's supposed to be about things like love and beauty, but you've just dragged me through the shit, and it's not fair. I'm not a criminal, nor is Ro - .' He stopped in terror.

Canon Byatt-Woods got up with a sigh. 'You are clearly over-wrought. We had best finish it there. You will come and see me tomorrow at prep. I shall expect an apology for that unseemly outburst, and I shall expect you to give me the rest of that name. Remember this, Moriston, while he is still walking the streets, other children may be at risk.'

As he showed the boy out, switched off the light and locked up, he added, 'Doctor Miles will be doing his sick bay calls tomorrow, so I shall get him to examine you. Report to Medical Room at ten in the morning, and do not speak to any of the other boys about this conversation. In the meantime, I commend to you the prayer for purity which you will find in your Confirmation Book. Prayer, Moriston, is a great healer...'

\*

Running upstairs in the boarding house, he bumped into the last person he wanted to see.

'Hey, Morri, what's up? You look as if you've been - .' Fillingham had a very stentorian tone, now that his voice had begun to break.

'Eff off, will you?' said Moriston between his teeth, fled into his room and flung himself on the bed. The violent sobbing had begun again.

When he finally got to sleep, Canon Byatt-Woods appeared in his dream, leering at him. 'Did he use his tongue on you? What did he do with his tongue?' Twisting and turning, the boy awoke. His life was black and horrible now, as if he'd already been sent to hell. If

Roland would only come and take him away from this abominable place.

How discreet were Woodsie and co., in cases like this? They weren't going to approach his parents about it, but there was so much scandalous gossip in and around the Minster, it could be all over the school in no time at all and, before much longer, it would come even to Roland's ears, so that he would believe that he had been betrayed after all. This thought caused him more pain than the ordeal he had been put through.

*

'Just slip off your things,' said the doctor easily. 'This won't take very long. In the cricket team, are you? What's your strong point, then? Batting, bowling?'

But the boy maintained a stubborn silence, standing there in his underpants and socks, his heart beating.

The doctor was a genial man with sons of his own, but the Deputy Head's earnest instruction this morning had taken him aback: to examine a child who might have suffered some physical abuse (outside school, of course); and, as was the procedure in such instances, absolute secrecy was to be observed. Even the boy was to be left in ignorance about the true purpose of the inspection.

The doctor took up his stethoscope. The comforting litany of 'breathe in... breathe out...' took over for a while. Then it was time for the eyes, ears, nostrils and mouth to be studied. The doctor spent a lot of time looking in the mouth and down the throat, saying 'Ah-hah' every so often. The boy tried unsuccessfuly not to shake.

'Better drop those down now, laddie. Right, just stand quite still for me.'

A huge warm hand cradled his genitals, while the doctor, his face uncomfortably close, said, 'Any aches or pains here?' He smelt of pipe tobacco.

Appalled by this sudden assault, the boy could only shake his head and let his breath out noisily.

'Right, young man, turn around. Touch your toes for me, and stay as you are.' A small gasp indicated that the man had got down on one knee. 'Any pain or discomfort at all, in the back passage?'

Moriston straightened up and spun round, his hands clamped over his private parts. His face was scarlet, and tears were pouring down it and splashing on to his chest.

'Why, laddie, there's no need to get upset. I've only just been doing a routine inspection.'

It wasn't routine, he thought, as he struggled back into his clothes, it was like rape, and far worse than any so-called molestation could ever have been. Roland only ever acted out of love. In his dismay he sank, half-dressed, on to a chair, and put his head in his hands.

'Now, is there something you feel you want to tell me?' said the doctor in his kindliest tone.

The boy's grief exploded and he began rocking to and fro, gibbering incomprehensible things.

'If it's any consolation at all,' said the doctor, 'I have found nothing amiss here, physically, but… Are you eating and sleeping all right? No, I thought maybe not. You're a bit pale and peaky. Not a case for sick bay, but perhaps just a little medication will help you along. Don't worry, I know how uptight boys get when exams are imminent. My own two were much the same!'

\*

'I have thought a great deal about what you told me yesterday,' said the Canon gravely, 'and I have made two decisions. Firstly, there is no need for any of this to be divulged to another person. In that way, the harm can be better contained. I have had a word with Mr Thorpe, and he has assured me that, as far as he is concerned, the matter goes no further. I have not bothered the Headmaster with it…'

The boy sat looking at him as if cowed into submission. 'Yes, sir.' At least it meant that Byatt-Woods had abandoned his quest for Roland's name.

'The doctor reports that you do not seem to have suffered any physical trauma, so my task is to help to limit your moral and mental distress. In this instance one must, I fear, be cruel to be kind. Until the end of this term, therefore, when you leave us - and this is my second decision, - you will be confined to the school buildings only. You will not attempt to communicate with anyone outside, and all letters addressed to you here will be read before being passed on to you. The same will happen to any that you may write, yourself. Do you understand?'

The boy, who was staring vacantly at the floor, nodded.

'You will also be excluded from the choir from now on.'

Moriston jerked his head up. 'Oh but sir, you can't do that!'

'If you first met this man in the Minster, then it is plain common sense to debar you from any further chances of seeing him. In any case, your voice is near to breaking, isn't it?'

'It's not fair. I can still get the top notes. You can't sack me, just like that. I've worked very hard in the choir, and - ' he clutched at any reed for support, ' - besides, I need the holiness of the services, after what I've been through. And I'm really sorry for what I said yesterday, sir. I was very upset.'

Canon Byatt-Woods had been looking closely at him during all this. 'Very well, you may continue as chorister, *pro tempore,* as long as I hear no adverse criticism of you. If, for instance, you became emotional during a service, I should have to reconsider. Oh yes, and there is one important liturgical point, which you have just reminded me of.'

'Sir?'

'One is permitted to take Communion only if one is truly penitent. Do you understand what I mean?'

He gave up the struggle of trying to put his side of it, faced as he was by a priest and a doctor who had profaned a beautiful thing, turning the whole experience with Roland into something sordid and horrible, as if they were two devils to be cast out.

*

I walked out of the door in the west front, across the little grassy square outside, through the medieval gate which divided the Close from the secular world beyond, and paused by the window of the gift-shop where, a million years ago, I had seen him standing next to another boy, waiting for me. Today, there were a few visitors loitering about, but no boys in blue blazers and caps. With a searing feeling, I entered the tea-shop and ensconced myself in our usual corner.

In bereavement, the most agonising thing is having to watch everyone else carry on their lives as normal, oblivious to the private sufferings of the lonely person nearby. An elderly waitress, whom I had not seen before, came over. I ordered tea, scones and cakes for two. When she looked at me with a question on her face, I merely said, 'It's all right. He'll be here in a moment.'

I could not stop blaming myself for what had happened. Something that should have been golden had turned to lead in my hands, and Piers would be as much the loser as I. However much I sought a solution to equal the simple ingenuity of furnishing the spare key in the first place, I was frustrated at every turn. We could not safely communicate with one another any more, and I had no idea how much the people at his school might have found out. I did not even know if it was safe for me to go on appearing in public, like this.

The tea-room was filling up, but the other chair at my table was still vacant. The waitress tottered back with a loaded tray, and noisily dumped its contents, item by item, on the table. 'Hope you don't mind if I ask you to settle now, sir,' she said. 'As it's getting busy, like.'

I dropped a five pound note on the table. She picked it up and went away. The figure of a man approached and sat down opposite me. I did not have the heart to point out that I already had two of everything on my table. The sub-organist took out a handkerchief and mopped his brow.

I saw my chance. 'Tell me, what has happened to Piers Moriston? It seems he is no longer allowed out.'

The man looked at me with dark-brown eyes, like those of a dog. 'Moriston,' he said, 'has been a naughty boy and is being kept in. If you are waiting for him to join you, you will wait a long time.'

There was a strange whirring sound in my ears, a humming inside my head, and a sudden pain lashed out at me, as if I had been hit. When I had recovered enough from this to open my eyes, the chair opposite me was empty. In disbelief, I reached over and felt the seat, but it was cool, polished and unbearably vacant. Piers should have been there, but I had betrayed him into the hands of our enemies, and my punishment was that, despite all my efforts to keep him, he was gone.

*

The following day, I sat in my usual place in the Minster, willing him to look my way, the merest glance from him being all I needed, to lift me out of the dark, desolate mood which had descended, for my fevered mind was now convinced that he had turned, or *been* turned, against me. The Morning Eucharist took its usual relentless course, but it was just as that fearful Evensong had been: no eye contact, nothing.

When we reached the point, after the Gospel, where a priest delivered a short address from the altar steps, I noticed Piers' hands resting on his knees, two bulges beneath his cloak, while the wan light made his long pale fingers look yellow and disjointed as if part of an ancient statue of the crucified Christ.

In my sorrow and trouble I did not know where to turn, for comfort came neither from opposite, nor from Him above. I was prey now to surreal notions, urging me to believe that the past weeks had been just make-believe: everything had been a shadow. Piers had *seemed* to return my gaze, God had *seemed* to smile indulgently on us, we had *seemed* to enjoy a love affair outrageous enough to bring this great building tumbling down; whereas the reality had been nothing of the kind – I had never known the choirboy, nor he me. We had not met in tea-shop, car, cottage. It was all an illusion that had no place at all in present time.

Look at him, over there: young chorister, sitting demurely in his stall, waiting for the moment to stand and sing. How could you ever imagine him as a paramour, a lover to lie beside? These limbs were not made to give you joy, those lips not fashioned for you to kiss. Stand back, man, you have no place here, where innocence is on display.

But I had only to look down at the ring, to know the truth of all those things which had happened with him on whom my eyes now rested. I had tasted that flesh, roused it to moments of ecstasy, I had shared a week in paradise with the lovely boy over there, and he had responded in every way, had even led me forward. Had not a warm, agile body come slipping into my bed, so that the marriage could be made truly complete? It *was* complete, as far as it had been allowed to go, and I was now waiting with bated breath to see if it had withstood the ravages of a society that does not allow such a love as Piers and I had for one another.

The priest (the very one who held the boy captive) began the prayer of consecration, and I knew that we were close to the moment of revelation. In this electric atmosphere, it was crucial that we should both repeat that special, private sacrament of the Cup with one another – if only to show that our bond had not been shattered after all.

I heard the dry voice, emerging as if from a great distance, inviting choir and people to come and take Communion, and there was a scuffling as the choir got up and hurried off to the altar. *He* always led off, on his side, and was usually kneeling at the altar rail almost before I had a chance to follow him with my eyes. Today it was different. He had slewed round in his seat, to let other boys past him. When they had gone, he knelt and put his face in his hands. So that was it. His soul had been poisoned against me, after all. I covered my eyes with hands that were soon wet with silent tears. My last hope was gone, and the day had turned black and bitter.

Then, like an inspiration from heaven, I saw, with awful clarity, the thought which must have been in my mind all along: bothered by what a casual acquaintance with that lad over there had developed into, *I was relieved that he had been found out.* I had allowed Fate to get me into this business, and it was her duty to see me out of it again. Or was it Fate that had moulded our affair? I could not thrust away the suspicion that Piers had been manipulating it from that very first glance which passed between us. If that were so, then his apparent imprisonment was the only way to salvation for him, whatever raw feelings it might produce in us both. Piers, safely confined to the school until the end of term, would suffer no further harm, and would doubtless very quickly forget.

Other members of the congregation were getting up all around me, but I did not budge. I could not bring myself to commit what had become a meaningless act. Rubbing my eyes, I stared over at him. He knelt with three or four of the little boys who had not yet been confirmed. Piers, look up, look across. You know I'm here. Whatever the risk to us both, give me some hope!

The Choir was almost deserted at this point, the choristers and men having not yet begun to file back. Members of the congregation were already moving eastwards to form that familiar double line which would shuffle slowly forwards. It's safe. *Do it now, Piers.*

Often during our time together, he or I would say something, only to hear the other exclaim, 'That's just what I was thinking about!' Our closeness was not only physical, our shared ideas not only spoken, we undoubtedly often saw one another's mind at work.

At that very moment, he parted his hands, tilting his head a little, and I saw two dark-grey eyes give me a brief but intense look, before being hidden from view again. It lasted only a fraction of a second, but the power of that look sent a shaft of warmth right through me. Everything was all right. His refusal to take Communion was a deliberate gesture of defiance - towards the priests, perhaps, who waited with wafers and Cup at the altar rail - , and a carefully calculated move, designed to leave me in no doubt. 'Don't give up hope,' the look had said. 'I'm a prisoner, but I haven't forgotten you.' Nothing mattered now – the missed rendezvous, the downcast eyes as he marched through the cloister. He had had to erect defences, he was under siege, but he got through to me, after all. And the message was still the same!

Wisely, he did not look across again but, at the end of the service, as the loud organ notes heralded the usual unaccompanied psalm, my overpowering sense of grateful relief found an echo in the bells pealing triumphantly from the west front.

*

He had looked for the Mercedes during practice, had seen it draw up in its usual place. How could he warn Roland that it was too easy to blow it? The vergers had almost certainly been put on special lookout, for Byatt-Woods was presiding today, and his eagle eye would be everywhere. Christ, Roland, you're too conspicuous, too recognisable. One stray glance from me, and they'll march you off. I can't even tell you why I can't come to you for tea any more – or for anything else, ever again.

He forced himself to keep his eyes down, forced himself to simulate singing, though he could not bring forth a single note today. He heard the boys and men all around uttering words with a cruel irony to them: "Blessed is he that cometh in the name of the Lord". The voices blended, rose to a triumphant climax: "Hosanna in the Highest". He felt a wave of nausea coming on, and fought it.

Boys pushed past him, glowering at him, but he ignored them, let them all go off to the altar. Filly, stupid idiot, with his mincing walk. And… God, Roland's still over there. He isn't going up either, which means we must both be unrepentant. Then so be it, and sod all the rest of them.

Even as these thoughts coursed through his mind, he heard the voice saying, "You have done wrong, you have done wrong". Perhaps that was true, after all, but Woodsie must have been bluffing when he said Roland would drop him, because he *hadn't* gone away, he was sitting opposite his boy as usual, up in the stall over there, probably trying to work out what was going on, and plotting a spectacular rescue…

As they filed back into the cloisters, he was dead scared he'd find Roland again – the very man he was fighting to protect – planted right by the door, exactly as he'd been after Evensong the other day, just standing there, as conspicuous as if he'd flung all his clothes off, on the very afternoon when Byatt-Woods was duty gaoler!

He felt his face go hot again, felt the tears beginning to burn and smart in his eyes – but, to his relief, the passage and cloister were empty today. The man he loved was so near, and yet so utterly far! He'd allowed himself a quick peep between his fingers, and had seen Roland looking across. Did he understand? Surely he'd see what the set-up was, now.

On the march back into school, Moriston finally gathered what was going on: Woodsie knew very well who this man was, but he didn't dare do anything, because it would cause a scandal and show up the school in a bad light. Conniving bastard!

*

The acrid smell of burning filled my nostrils, and smoke stung my eyes. Only a gaunt brick chimney stack was left standing, which had once served both the lounge and the space upstairs devoted to stored items of sentimental value. One line of wall, near where the front door had been, was daubed with white paint, accusing me of doing a bestial act with a boy… The message was absurdly plain: we had been spotted, and this was the reward for our tenderness and constancy.

I awoke, quite upset by the violence and reality of it, and disturbed by the implication that my conscience had been wrestling with me. Aschenbach had a dream about debauchery. Was this any better?

Hoping to find some consolation even in a pointless action, I got up, dressed and, without bothering to have breakfast, drove straightway out to the cottage, only to find it intact, lifeless, stale and depressing. I sought solace in the two photos of Piers on the wall in my bedroom, but they were nothing more than portraits of a becoming young stranger whose expression seemed to combine pity with scorn. In the grip of an overwhelming desire to possess my boy again, I could understand how one killed one's beloved, to prevent him from belonging to anyone else.

Outside, the wind whipped the waves up a grey beach, bringing back to me the image of Piers buried in the sand. Alone with my misery, I wandered up to the lumber room, found the locked casket containing Mother's effects and rummaged through it, as though expecting to find that it had been rifled. There was a crucifix covered in mother-of-pearl, a necklace of rhinestones she'd been especially fond of, her watch, one or two faded letters from Father and a bottle of the powerful painkillers she'd had to use during her last agonising weeks. As I looked at these pathetic objects, my eyes filled with tears, but whether they were for my dead mother, my lost love or myself, I could not tell.

I do not know what it was that urged me to go into the room in which Piers had briefly slept during his stay, unless it was merely to punish myself further. It was like a prison cell, the bed stripped of its covers, the rest of the room devoid of all ornaments. I opened the doors of his wardrobe, as if in hope that he might have left some item of his clothing behind. The hangers were empty, the shelves bare. It was as if a judgment had been passed on us both. And, at that moment, I believed that, even if I were foolish enough to proceed with my purchase of "Stella Maris", I would never *own* it, any more than I would ever see Piers in private again.

After leaving the cottage, I went back twice to check every window and door, in case I had left a weak spot which some malicious spirit might find and exploit.

*

'Sir, Moriston's blubbing again.'

On the film they had just been shown, sweethearts and married couples were torn apart as the men went off to war, and there, in close-up, was a ring on the finger of a woman as she embraced her departing husband…

'Sh, Fillingham, what have you been told to do when that happens?'

'Leave him alone, sir.'

'That's right, then he'll get over it more quickly.'

'Is it true he's having a breakdown, sir?'

He heard it all, and recognised Byatt-Woods' astuteness in putting it about that Moriston was being kept indoors because he had a nervous disorder and had to live quietly. If only they knew that his emotion was a powerful amalgam of defiance, anger and despair, as well as grief! He could not get Roland out of his thoughts. How was he coping, if in fact he understood? He might always be over there on the other side of the Choir, but he didn't seem to be showing any attempt to find a loophole for them to have even the briefest meeting or talk, as though he'd chucked in the towel. Did affairs usually tail off like this?

Alone, the door locked to his room, where he spent all the time that was not devoted to singing, choir practice or school lessons, he pondered for a long time how to contact Roland, and finally decided to write him a note, which he would leave up in his stall for him to find. It was monstrously difficult to write to someone he knew so intimately without sounding reproachful or girlish. The important thing was to explain why he was being kept in school, to say sorry for having missed their next meeting and ask him for an answer.

After he had finished it and signed off with "Much love, Piers", he read it through, his heart pounding. Would Roland be angry? He still kept on coming to services, so he couldn't have given it all up, not completely. Then an idea struck him: if he left the note in Roland's seat, it might be picked up by someone else and, like a grenade, explode in their faces.

With the help of the big French dictionary from the school library, he laboriously cobbled together a version which he hoped would confound anyone else, should they chance to see it:

*"Cher R,*

> *Depuis que je suis atrapé revenant dans l'école après notre rendezvous, je suis tenu prisonnier ici par notre Député (le prêtre avec les cheveux gris – attention avec lui!). J'ai été très soigneux ne pas te révéler, mais j'ai besoin (très grand) te revoir. Tu peux mettre une réponse ici où tu trouve ceci? C'est dommage je ne pouvais pas venir au rencontre avec toi, mais tu vois maintenant pourquoi. Je pense tout le temps à nous.*
>
> *Avec beaucoup d'amour, P."*

He knew it must have mistakes, but he dared not show it to his French teacher and, in any case, Roland would be able to understand it. Maybe he'd write his answer in French! He added a P.S.: *"Écris moi en français. C'est plus sauf!"*

The next afternoon, just before Evensong, he excused himself from the Song School under the pretext of needing the loo urgently ('it's these pills the doctor's given me, sir'), and darted down the spiral staircase, past the vestries and through the side entrance into the Choir. There was nobody about. Like a ferret, he scurried up to the canon's stall where Roland always sat, plopped down on the cushion and was filled with a power and warmth he hadn't known since they parted. If only *he* could know that his boy had sat here on his seat!

The bell began ringing for Evensong, he put the envelope containing his note on the wooden ledge where the hymn and prayer books were neatly spaced out. The whiteness of the paper was startling against the dark polished oak. He picked it up and tucked it under a hymn book, with just the edge showing.

Footsteps sounded nearby, in a sudden panic he retrieved his note, stuffed it in his pocket and started back the way he had come. As he reached the exit from the Choir, there was Canon Byatt-Woods, blocking his retreat. 'What are you doing here all on your own, Moriston? Why are you not at practice in the Song School?'

'I was taken short, sir.' He wished his face wouldn't colour up like that.

'Get yourself to the vestry and robe up. The others are already there,' said the priest sternly, and turned on his heel.

The boy was sorely tempted to make a dash for it, into the south transept, out of the door and, hopefully, into Roland's arms. An *abduction* was called for, as never before!

But Roland did not attend Evensong that day. The stall was occupied by some old biddy whom Piers had never seen before and hoped never to see again. He spent the whole service thanking his lucky stars he hadn't left his note, after all. The possiblity that he was losing Roland, or had lost him already, rose up in him like a monster.

He vainly racked his brains for another, safer way of getting through to him. He could not use the payphone, because there were always too many bodies around it, and secrecy was impossible.

The organ postlude began, Squires, next to him, was giving him a nudge. Filly on the other side was already up on his feet, looking at him to follow suit. He'd missed his cue. 'Get moving, boy!' one of the choirmen behind hissed at him.

They processed out and round to the choir vestry. As Moriston was removing his robes, Dr Hutley came up to him. 'You aren't pulling your weight, are you? The Magnificat was a mess. You muffed both the entries, and Squires and Togher were right up the creek. If you don't pull your finger out, I shall be telling Mr Baines.'

He swallowed. 'Sorry, sir. The fact is, I'm not very well.'

'If you aren't well,' said the sub-organist tartly, 'don't sing. Report sick. Next, I suppose, you'll be ducking out of rehearsals for the concert.'

\*

Cursing my stupidity, I was forced to stop the car two streets away from the Minster, where a passer-by found me tottering about on the pavement and escorted me to a surgery nearby. By chance, the doctor was available.

'Sorry to be so much trouble. I've never felt on the point of passing out like this before.'

The doctor examined my eyes. 'Have you banged your head recently, at all?'

'No, not to my knowledge.'

'Are you doing a very stressful job, perhaps? You look a bit peaky.'

I explained that I could fit my work in to suit myself.

The doctor tested my blood pressure, listened to my breathing and looked inside my ears.

A distant bell began to sound. 'I was just on my way to Evensong…'

'Better give it a miss today. You'll have other opportunities to hear our angelic boys sing.' He was writing out a prescription. 'There's a chemist round the corner. I advise you to get back home and go to bed for twenty-four hours. If you are still suffering from giddiness after that, come back and see me again, Mr Millan. Might be a good idea to take a holiday, if you can, right away from this town. Wish I could do the same, with all this lovely hot weather!'

*

The clock struck ten, as if a man were being hanged up in the grim castle keep beyond the square where he and Roland had first spoken to one another. A kid, younger than he was, had been boasting in front of the bigger ones, had announced his 'coming of age' for tonight, and the seniors would be gathered round to watch him perform, before the final stroke died away – a time-honoured Wharnley Choir School custom, a circus act, with Filly as the ringmaster.

The injustice of it struck him: they got away with it, when it was dirty but, when it was marvellous and special – with a person you really loved – you got hauled over the coals. *I came into your bed, I gave you a ring with our names on it.*

He did not yet know, at this stage, how all these matters would colour his view of relationships in later life but, already, the tantalising quality of his present existence was beginning to harden him. In his long periods alone, his mind kept coming back to Roland and his apparent inability (or was it refusal?) to do something to help. Christ, he cut Evensong today, and he had become unreachable. What to do? The term was racing along now.

I once believed that he could work magic, that he could do anything – he gets ciné film processed specially, in time for us to see, he's driven his Merc all the way from Geneva to Wharnley. He's going to buy his own cottage by the sea, and leave it to me, later on. He can draw, paint, take stunning photos (and develop and print them himself), he designs operas, restores burnt-out mansions – and he's a fantastic bloke in bed. *But he can't get me out of this bloody place...*

He sat, miserably comparing all this to the pathetic Valete they'd already got him to write for the magazine: senior chorister, took part in two or three recordings of church music, cross-country, swimming, cricket, piano; place at Keatwells in Dorset (provided they didn't put a spanner in the works at the last minute).

He knew he would never have Roland's dash, his charisma, the subtle scent of daring and danger he carried about with him. Couldn't he, the magician, have done something to save their ruined affair? There was anger in him, and hurt, because it now looked as if Roland didn't want him any more. If he was still coming to services, it must mean only one thing: he'd chosen another boy, was waiting to make an approach, to secure another *catamite* (he'd found the word in a thesaurus during prep).

Then, like a smack in the face, a memory came back to him: Roland was after Filly. He'd asked about him at the cottage. Filly was handsome, Filly was sexually ready now (unlike himself, still stuck with dry runs, night after bloody night). Roland would probably take Filly off to the cottage for the summer hols, and they'd make whoopee together – all the way.

He slumped to the floor, rested his head against the bed and wailed his heart out. Roland was just a dirty old man after all, a boy-chaser, like Woodsie had said, and he deserved to be denounced. Horrified by the thought, he staggered to his feet again. From their very first encounter, Roland had always seemed so steadfast, someone who would never cut this special knot they had tied. But then he was also an experienced person with his own life to lead, and he'd had other male relationships before. He wouldn't want to keep one boy in tow for ever. Moriston today, Fillingham tomorrow, and heaven knew how many after that.

Half-way to his door something stopped him, turned him round and, to his own amazement, got him down on his knees. He tried to pray for the strength to fight his resentment towards Roland, who once said he believed God was on their side, despite everything. Whether it was the doctor's tablets, or whether he indeed got an answer, a comfortable sensation infused him, with a calming of the brain. He would write, in affection, a letter of gratitude which, even if nothing else ever happened between them, would prove that a vestige of their love, however battle-scarred by now, was still alive.

The next morning, he stopped Squires. 'I've got an errand for you. Top secret, mind. You are to post these.' He handed two envelopes, fully addressed, to the younger boy, who studied the inscriptions and said, 'Mr R. Millan – is that - ?'

'Shut up, you little fool,' Piers hissed at him.

' – the man,' Squires went on inexorably, but in an undertone, 'who came and asked me who you were?'

'You breathe one word of this to anyone, and I'll kill you!'

Squires looked at him with his innocent blue eyes. 'What's it worth?' He was given a pound note to pay for postage, 'and keep the rest.'

'Bloody hell!' said the child, and ran off before the senior could change his mind. Moriston had been behaving very strangely of late...

That evening, the school was buzzing as never before with a new rumour, and boys clustered round a neatly-typed new announcement pinned to the main notice board: "Dr E.J.Hutley, with the agreement of the Headmaster and Governors, has left in order to collect material for a book about French medieval organs." What the notice did not say, but what was in everyone's mouth, was that Hutters had been copped at last, *in flagrante,* and that his 'tour of France' was to be indefinitely prolonged. In fact, he wouldn't be coming back. That evening, Moriston was unusually elated.

\*

I was conscious as never before of a distortion of the timescale. The daily round flowed past me like a speeded-up film, whereas my time spent alone – the fitful nights especially – was remorselessly strung-out. I lived a robotic existence, dressing, eating, undressing, aware only of the pointlessness of it all. I had brought my restoration project to an abrupt end, I avoided the cottage like the plague, and my stage designs remained untouched, for my muse had quite deserted me.

I had also abandoned my exciting but perilous habit of placing myself in his path, for it was too painful to take up a station of love, only to be ignored by my boy.

When only two weeks of the summer term remained, I began to get impatient. As if locked in a custom I could not break out of, I was still a faithful witness at each service, though he never looked at me across the Choir any more. I had to be content, merely to be near him, and to know that he was aware of my presence, though the suspicion was fast growing in me that all the love and affection, his radiant sexuality, even, had simply withered away.

He was strangely static, statuesque even, he never fidgeted as he had done in the past, his hands were still when he was not holding music – those hands which had touched and loved me! I wanted him, needed desperately to drive him away to a safe, secluded place where we could release our mutual desire again. My frenzy plunged me into despair, for it was worse than if we had never come together in the first place. The treasure had been given, thrust into my willing hands, and then wrenched away again. Surely he must be thinking and feeling the same?

When the fleeting passage of days had almost reached its conclusion, I bought a ticket for the musical concert to be held on the evening before school broke up. It was an expensive seat, in the second row of the nave, commanding a good view of the choral society singers arranged in tiers beneath the Crossing, in front of the screen. As the choir came in, (the boys in their uniforms), the sunlight was playing in the north transept and up in the lantern tower. Beyond the dark brown organ case with its gleaming pipes, the vaulted roof of the Choir was in a greenish gloom.

He was prominent in the centre of the line of boys down in front. Pale face, dark eyes looking down, the brown hair fluffy, boyish, his sensitive fingers holding the music. I closed my eyes as the harmonies blended and swelled, the organ lending colour and piquancy to a piece by Duruflé. This was the last time I would see my boy sing, though his voice was lost among the others, that low, musical voice which I so loved, and which would soon break. Little game would become big game, and the youth would scorn the man, grow away, forgetting the ring he had bought me, to seal our compact.

I already felt as though someone had died and, in my mind's eye, saw his sand-streaked body, as I had pulled it from the collapsed tunnel, wishing now that it had really happened, so that I could keep him like that for ever.

The boy, in his exposed position, was both flattered and aghast to see Roland there, right in front. Whenever he raised his hand to his chin, there was a glint of metal on his ring finger. Had he got the letter? God, Byatt-Woods was sitting just across from him in the front row! Suddenly, he hated Roland, wanted to scream it out, there and then, in the presence of everyone, for he was certain he was favouring Filly with his looks. Waves of nausea began to rise in him.

In truth I allowed most of the programme which they sang to pass over my head, which was having one of its silly turns. I came back to myself, with a start, only when the last item began, for a piano and small orchestra had materialised and were accompanying the chorus with strident chords and complex percussive rhythms. I closed my eyes. At Jonathan's insistence, we visited the fresh grave on our way from Greece. Flame-red flowers in the sunlight, as harsh as the music which now rang in my ears, a plain white wooden cross with

"Stravinski Igor" painted in black and, already, the pencilled signatures of admirers. Nearby, an iron grille allowed a glimpse through the wall of a muddy little inlet of the lagoon. Venice was no place of triumph for me.

The music, having worked itself up into a fury, subsided into a long, tranquil melody of great beauty. The voices, with their endlessly repeated "Laudate" phrases, caressed the notes, sliding from one to another like waves, down the scale a little, then back, the whole supported by bold chords from the piano, softer ones from the orchestra.

I looked up into the lantern, to the point where, seventy feet or so above the pavement, an open gallery ran round. I saw the man up there, his fair hair caught in the sunlight, his face looking down at the back of a boy in a black hooded cope, saw him hesitate, and then fling himself down into the Crossing. Seventy feet, and a bump which seemed to make the Minster floor shake. The boy turned, looked, and then ran, his cope and cassock flying out behind, to the spot where his lover lay still. A broken hand with a shining metal ring rested on the pavement.

But then my attention was jolted back to the scene before me. I had heard, as surely as I had just witnessed that vision, Piers' voice detach itself for an instant from the rest, as it turned on a note and began its lovely downward path again. Sweet, pure and haunting, as I had always imagined it to be. I looked at him. He was staring down at his music, but he had surely meant that moment of delight to be for his lover. The work was approaching its end, but I could contain my emotion no longer, and got up to flee. As I reached the end of the broad aisle that ran westwards down the crowded nave, my sobs broke loose, loud and echoing against the final hushed chord.

Faces turned to look in surprise, people made a shushing noise and, from his vantage point, the boy saw the man caught in the great bars of colour which the sun projected down from the west window, his sorrow made public, his bitter grief displayed in pitiful fashion for all the world to witness. For the first time, he was disgusted by Roland, his sick feeling boiled up and over and, in the second or two of silence after the music died away, he vomited, loudly and copiously.

My craven exit was mercifully drowned in the applause, as I reached the door at last, thankful for the empty vestibule beyond, where I could put my forehead against the cold dark stone and let my emotion run its violent course, my hands clutching at the wall with its grimy carvings, as if to break off a piece to take with me as a talisman. Piers, I am done for...

\*

I lay soaked in perspiration between rumpled sheets, my head on a pillow that seemed to be made of rock. Although my window was open, the heat in the room, together with the thoughts churning inside my head, gave me no rest, as if I were clamped in the grip of a fiend from one of those paintings of the Last Judgment. Getting up, I sat by the window, the hot breath from the street beating in on my naked body. The sky was not quite dark, although the Minster bell had long since sounded midnight, and a few stars penetrated the hazy atmosphere.

I rested my head in my hand, trying to doze, but pictures, sensations and ideas continued to spin in a confused tangle: I saw, in brilliant colours, the boy on the horse, saw his first smile in the greenish light of the transept, saw the thousand expressions in his eyes.

'Would things have been different, if you'd had him all the way through?' That was his voice, talking about Father. Perhaps, but then there would have been no Barry, no Jonathan, no Piers. There was some small solace in the thought that I had broken new ground, charted a forbidden territory and yet survived to tell the tale.

He came along the shore line, his bare feet washed by the waves that foamed up  over the smooth sand. 'Don't you care about what happens to me?'

He was wearing the Bermudas, and as he came to a halt near me, he took up a nonchalantly graceful pose.

'Of course, but you'll be all right.' You'll come out of it unscathed.

'I shall probably get married.' Said with emphasis.

The dim light in the sky was turning imperceptibly to the unearthly colour which precedes dawn. Freezing now, I fetched a blanket, wrapped myself in it and sat by the window again.

There was no sound from inside or outside the house. It might have been a silent and sacred moment, like the one when Piers woke me to watch the sun rising. But Piers was not with me: my room, my bed and my life were empty now. I hated this room, hated the whole place where I had chosen to lodge, and came to a quick decision: I would give my landlady a month's rent, clear out of here today, sort a few things at the cottage and return to Switzerland.

As the dawn crept up outside, however, I began to feel differently. There had been a signal from him, yesterday evening, and I had foolishly ignored its meaning. *He let his voice detach from the others, just for me!*

I bathed, shaved and dressed, slowly and carefully, choosing the same light grey suit which I had been wearing when he first smiled at me beneath the watchful eyes of four bishops and, as the early sunlight played on my form in the mirror, I was almost elated. The man before me was not one who had suffered a loss, but one about to go to a festival, a celebration, an occasion for rejoicing, even. As the sun warmed on my face, I suddenly had a vision: Piers, carrying his case, walked out of the school, and instead of getting into the taxi, made straight for me: a simple action, a step to freedom, and the priest would be left behind, powerless!

I prepared myself some breakfast, packed up all my things, explained to my astonished landlady that I was unexpectedly called away, and strode out to my car, as if chains had fallen from my body. This was not an end at all, but a new beginning. Far above, the sun was shining on the angel on the roof of the Choir.

*

The heat was overpowering, and his clothes stuck to his body as he stood on the uneven pavement opposite the school. There were some old wrought-iron railings bordering a front garden just here, and he leaned against them, staring obliquely across at the vast front door with its faded red paint, trying to fight the giddiness which had come over him again, when he got out of the car a few yards up the street, to take up his position.

There was a ringing in his ears, too, and the sounds of traffic and people's footsteps echoed as if at several removes from him. He was in the street, but he saw and heard it as though at the end of a tunnel. His eyes recorded two school doors, which constantly converged and separated again.

The railings, hard spears in his back, were the only reality. The flower in his buttonhole seemed to have grown to the size of a large chrysanthemum, so urgent was its signalling redness below his chin.

Someone stopped and spoke to him, but whether it was to ask if he was all right, or merely to inquire the way, he had no idea. He kept his gaze fixed rigidly on that door, through which *he* must come. The person went away again.

He had wondered how he might get his foreign address to Piers, but could find no safe method of doing it. Nor could he ask at the school for *his* address, without stirring up a hornet's nest. In the end, he had telephoned the school secretary to find out what time the boys would be released, and she told him, as if he were an uncle or parent, someone quite trustworthy.

Although the street was quiet, and everything seemed oddly remote today, he still felt exposed, pinned here beneath the pitiless sun like a sacrifice awaiting the end. He longed for a shadow to cover him. When they opened the great door across the street and stepped out, they would see nothing else but his buttonhole flaring like a beacon. He heard Piers' laughter, like water, and looked up quickly. But there was nothing: grimy, faceless windows looked down, and the door remained implacably shut.

He made himself helplessly drunk when Mother died, trying to insulate himself from a grief which threatened to carry him off also. In a less extreme way, he felt the same again, for the heat, and his lack of sleep, were telling on him. The railings hurt his back, but he dared not stir.

They would come out of the door, whooping and running to taxis or their parents' cars, pausing only for seconds to look his way, to register that this was the man who had run, sobbing, from last night's concert. In all the rush, Piers might not even see him, though he would surely expect him to be there. *He had always been there*, always in the line of sight, when *his* eyes swept along, seeking.

He looked at his watch. When the bell next struck, the door would open. Already, a taxi cab was crawling along on the far side. Early, but ready. Was this one for *him*, then? A simple matter of bribing the driver to change his route and Piers would, as always, play along with it, rejoicing no doubt at his lover's audacity.

More cars came inching up to the school. Luckily, his view of the door and the pavement immediately in front of it was not masked. He could not have moved to another spot if he had tried.

Then a window was opened somewhere up near the roof of the school and three cheers sounded, in shrill boys' voices. The half-hour began to chime, the red door was flung back, and they came out, some in uniform, some already in casual clothes, jostling, rushing for the taxis, squabbling as to whose was which. A case burst open, its contents spilled out and were trampled by dozens of feet. Engines raced, in warning of trains to be caught.

His vision and hearing both became crystal clear, as if he had been struck cold sober. He panicked, unable to see Piers, nor to know if he might have missed him. He did not even know how many boarders there were, whether more were still to come. Sweat poured down his face and dripped from his chin. *Where was he?* Not still a prisoner? He must come now, must come across the street to his lover, and to release. He was buoyed up with expectancy and longing, incapable of ceding defeat.

The taxis had moved off, along with the last of the private cars. The door was closed again. The three-quarters chimed and, at last, the hour – eleven long, booming notes that went through his head like cannonballs.

He had missed Piers, then: he had left earlier, been smuggled away to the station in the same early morning light which had brought a fond man such hope. There was no point in staying here now. Nothing kept him, nor would ever bring him back. He could not tell if the desolate emptiness was in or around him. He felt faint and sick.

A taxi sped round the corner, pulled up smartly outside the school, and the door opened once more. The boy had his black polo neck sweater and jeans on, the man was glad to see, but he looked very much younger than when he had worn them before. He was in shadow, but the extreme whiteness of his complexion was unmistakeable. He paused on the pavement, and the priest came out, took his case and, in a gesture of finality, began to carry it to the taxi.

Piers stood still, and his observer knew that he would never forget how he looked, as if he himself were the camera to capture that fraction of a second, as though the man on the beach were answering his Summoner. The boy's eyes were looking down at the road, his long slender hands at his sides and yet, even in that quiet posture, there was something of spirit and defiance.

He was conscious of Byatt-Woods at his side, and of the man standing expectantly on the other side of the street, and he felt caught between the two of them, torn apart by two absolutely irreconcilable truths. He knew and obeyed his duty to protect Roland, but he was also ashamed, because he had been made to feel like that. He didn't need that man over there any more: he had outgrown him. Nonetheless, as he climbed into the taxi, it was with a momentary tearing remorse as though, after all they had been through together, he had stabbed his lover in the back.

His tongue would not move, he could not breathe, much though he wanted desperately to call his beloved boy over to him, and to hell with the priest. Piers slowly raised his eyes, and they dwelt for an instant on his lover, who raised a hand, to signal, but the hand would not obey him: it rose to his mouth instead, as if to blow a farewell kiss.

Then Piers turned away, got in, and was driven rapidly away. A second later, the front door of the school slammed shut, and the street was empty again. The man was if paralysed, he could have flown to the top of the tower as soon as race to his car and drive off in pursuit.

The light which blazed down on the scene was less blinding than that which dawned at last on his weary brain. Piers had been turned away from him, did not want him any more. The burning sun was the eye of God upon him, announcing that he had committed an awesome sin, for which he was now paying very dearly. He had been fond of Piers, but had carried his fondness past acceptable limits, thinking to stave off the boredom which he feared more than anything else in his life. He had done nothing but delude himself over the past weeks since the boy had become lost to him.

Broken and exhausted, he dragged himself back to the car and, tears mingling with the sweat on his face, headed mechanically out of the town, towards the sea, his lips never ceasing to repeat that name: 'Piers, Piers, Piers', as though there could remain any consolation in it.

The cottage seemed even more unlived in and musty than on his last brief visit. There was a letter on the mat. He picked it up, went into the lounge and, without bothering to open the curtains, dropped into a chair. The writing on the envelope was familiar, he slowly opened it and unfolded the sheet of notepaper inside.

*Dear Roland, I am doing two copies of this, one to your rooms and one to the cottage, in case one does not arrive. Another boy is smuggling them out for me, as my letters are read now before they go. I'm very sorry I did not come to our meeting, but I am being guarded till the end of term. I had to see the Deputy Head (who is one of the priests) and he more or less blackmailed me*

*into talking about us. I was caught with the key when I got back*
*in. It was pretty awful and he was very severe. He said I was*
*wrong to go with you and tried to get me to say who you were,*
*but I wouldn't.*

*I'm still grateful to you, Roland, for our special friendship,*
*despite everything, and I will try to come and see you again some*
*time, when we've both got over it a bit. Mother and Father will*
*be home for the hols. I'd like you to have met them.*

*I hope you are well,*
*love, Piers.*

His hands trembled, he rested his aching head on the arm of the
chair, shaken again by the painful sobbing over which he had no
control. The letter was dated two days after their abortive
rendezvous, and the copy to his rooms in town must have gone
astray. If it had arrived before, he would have left the town there and
then, with all his hopes dashed.

As if the letter contained an instruction to that effect, he removed
the ring – *his* ring – from his finger, but his hands were shaking so
much that he dropped it, and it rolled under the settee.

He sat for a long time, reading and re-reading the letter, hoping to
find a more pleasant message between the lines. But the reality was
inescapable: the promise to meet up again was mere politeness, the
boy was gone for ever. They were guilty of a sin which would
remain with them both for the rest of their lives.

Like an old man, he went upstairs to his room and sat on the bed.
Piers, nude, looked down at him from the wall, and he turned his face
away. What could he do now? Even his decision to retreat to his
place in Switzerland held no comfort: he would never be able to
escape from himself.

In the bathroom he looked in the mirror, startled by what he saw.
The emotional switchback of the past few months had made its mark.
The face had aged, developed more lines, deeper lines, and the
darkness around the eyes was more intense, the eyes themselves
broken and bloodshot.

There was no consolation in the garden either, where a warm
breeze played among the flowers. The paddock was dismally empty,
and from the dunes came only the calling of gulls, as if to mock him.

Then a vision came to him – not Piers in the sand tunnel, but
Piers exposed to an inquisition, the priest probing, pinpointing,

reprimanding… Piers defenceless, protecting his lover at all costs, but selling himself at the same time. And, even as he watched, with an inward eye, he saw a figure approaching along the beach at night, bearing a flaming torch in its hand, which it hurled at the cottage, the keen wind helping the conflagration on its way, destroying everything in its path. Scraps of paper and charred material carried high into the air, the windows burst with loud cracking sounds, the roof gave up the ghost and tumbled in amid a shower of sparks, and everything that they had ever been to one another was obliterated in a holocaust of bitterness and shame.

The furious roaring of the fire was inside his head now, and the brilliance of the light on sea and sand made him screw up his eyes in pain. He wanted darkness, oblivion, a safe place in which to nurse his sorrow.

As if the grief had somehow detached his soul from its physical self, he saw the man standing facing the dunes, his head back, his fair hair shining in the sun. The mouth opened and closed, emitting no sound at first, but then, like the buffet of a great wave upon the shore, a fearful cry issued from his lips, bearing the anguish, torment and agony not of those few months, but of years, centuries, for as long as man has loved man: a cry of despair and defiance to the world, timeless, and borne on the breeze.